Callie challenged.

And so he did.
Hard.
Hot.
Hungry.
Those words barely hinted at the intensity of the kiss Jake gave Callie.

He murmured Callie's name, then nuzzled a slow, searing path to her throat. Her head fell back as he slid his mouth downward to mark the place where her pulse beat out an unmistakable message of excitement. Callie gave a soft cry. Her fingers winnowed slowly through the rough silk of his chest hair.

And then... And then it was over.
They eased back, broke apart. The distance between them went from nothing to nearly a foot.

"Y-you're still n-not my type," Callie whispered.

If Jake had had the breath, he might have laughed. Instead, he said, "I know, Callie. God help us both, I know."

Dear Reader,

June is a terrific month. It's the time of year when the thoughts of women—and men—turn to love...*and* marriage. Not only does June mark the beginning of those hot, lazy days of summer, it's also a month with a fantastic, fiery lineup from Silhouette Desire.

First, don't miss the sizzling, sensational *Man of the Month, The Goodbye Child* by Ann Major, which is the latest in her popular Children of Destiny series. Also in June, look for *The Best Is Yet To Come,* another story of blazing passion and timeless romance from the talented pen of Diana Palmer.

Rounding out June are four other red-hot stories that are sure to kindle your emotions written by favorite authors Carole Buck, Janet Bieber and—making their Silhouette Desire debuts—Andrea Edwards and Amanda Stevens.

So get out those fans and cool down...then heat up with stories of sensuous, emotional love—only from Silhouette Desire!

All the best,

Lucia Macro
Senior Editor

CAROLE BUCK

WHITE LACE PROMISES

SILHOUETTE *Desire*®

Published by Silhouette Books New York

America's Publisher of Contemporary Romance

SILHOUETTE BOOKS
300 East 42nd St., New York, N.Y. 10017

WHITE LACE PROMISES

ISBN: 0-373-05644-3

First Silhouette Books printing June 1991

Printed in the U.S.A.

One

───

Jake Turner wanted a room to rent. That much he knew for certain. But one of the many things he *didn't* know was whether driving his pickup around the back roads of Georgia during a torrential downpour was going to lead him to what he desired.

Jake leaned forward, his chest only an inch or two from the steering wheel. He peered out through the windshield, searching for something that would tell him where he was. Frowning, he mentally reviewed a portion of the telephone conversation he'd had with his prospective landlady, a Miss Henrietta Penelope Barnwell, earlier in the day.

"You say you saw our ad in the *Deacon's Crossing Weekly?*" she'd asked after he'd finished explaining his reason for calling. Her voice had been as soft and fluttery as a magnolia blossom in a breeze. "How nice! Now, I *do* hope you're not thinkin' we run some sort of boardin' establishment, because we most certainly do not. Not that we're inexperienced at this rentin' business. No, no. We've been doin' it off and on for, oh, must be nigh on to two

years now. We started after my darlin' brother passed away.
It's his room we rent out, you see. We bein' myself and my
dear niece, Callie. There's also Palmer Dean the Third. He's
my only nephew and Callie's half brother. He's the reason
we started rentin' out in the first place. He'll be goin' to
college before too long and well, let's just say every little bit
of income helps.''

Sensing that the loquacious old lady on the other end of
the line had to pause to draw breath, Jake had opened his
mouth to speak. He'd closed it several seconds later when it
became clear that Henrietta Penelope Barnwell had per-
fected the art of talking while inhaling.

''I'm afraid I don't recollect the exact phrasin' of what we
put in the paper,'' she'd apologized. ''But chances are you
didn't read what we intended, anyway. Augustus Bates—he
publishes the *Weekly*—probably changed things out of all
recognition to suit his so-called editorial judgment. It never
fails. Augustus Bates wouldn't leave well enough alone if it
was the Lord's own handiwork.''

''Miss Barnwell—'' he'd managed to wedge in at this
point.

''Are you a big man, Mr. Turner?'' she'd questioned
suddenly, giving no indication she'd registered his attempt
to stem the flow of her monologue.

''Uh...'' Jake had floundered, wondering what the hell
his size had to do with anything. For the record, he stood a
muscular six foot one. He'd never had any complaints about
his height or any other of his vital statistics.

''You sound as though you might be,'' Miss Barnwell had
gone on. ''Now, the room we're offerin' isn't teeny-tiny by
any means, but it might seem confinin' to a man with a lot
to stretch out. And while the servin's at our table aren't
skimpy— Oh, the ad in the paper *did* mention that break-
fasts and suppers come with the room, didn't it?''

''Ah—yes, ma'am.'' Jake hadn't been certain where the
ma'am had come from. It had simply slipped out and he'd
let it stand.

"It didn't say lunch, did it? There's no lunch, I'm afraid."

"No problem."

"Of course, I probably could pack you a bag lunch to take to your—your—what did you call it again?"

"Architectural restoration project," he'd supplied. "But I wouldn't put you to the trouble of making me lunch. I can fend for myself when it comes to meals." I can fend for myself when it comes to anything, he'd added silently, then continued. "As I told you before, your ad caught my eye because it said you're located in Deacon's Crossing. So's the site I'm working on. I was down here a few months ago for the same job and I ended up staying at a place called the Roadside Retreat Motel."

"Why, that's three towns over from here."

"Exactly."

"Well, we'd certainly be more convenient than *that.*"

There'd been a brief silence.

"I'd like to take a look at the room, Miss Barnwell," Jake had finally said, ignoring the small voice that told him he'd be much better off returning to the Roadside Retreat Motel.

"Oh, yes, of course," she'd agreed immediately. "But I'm afraid you'll have to wait on my niece comin' home. Callie has to be consulted before any final arrangements are made, you see. And I just *know* she's goin' to be late again tonight. Poor thing. She's been workin' herself to a frazzle lately. Why, she barely survived the prom season and already she's up to her elbows creatin' gowns for three-quarters of the competitors in this year's Miss Founders' Day Festival pageant. *And* she's gettin' pestered to death by Janie Mae Winslow about an ensemble for the upcomin' Peanut Princess contest. I swear, that Janie Mae is determined to flaunt herself like a road sign every chance she gets. But, back to your stoppin' by to see the room. Hmm. Let me see. How would seven-thirty this evening suit you, Mr. Turner?"

"Seven-thirty would be fine," Jake had affirmed, squelching the urge to ask what sort of ensemble an aspiring Peanut Princess might require. "I'll need directions."

"Directions?" Miss Barnwell had echoed. "Oh, dear. I'm afraid I'm not very good with directions. I don't drive, you see. My dear friend, Petal Conroy does, though, and she's gracious enough to offer me transportation whenever I need it. But... hmm. Directions. Well, you leave Deacon's Crossing goin' east. Or... is it west? Oh, never mind that. You drive out of town, goin' by our lovely little library. It's dedicated to the honor of an ancestress of ours, Miss Caroline Anne Barnwell. Callie's her namesake, by the way. It'll be on your... now wait, let me picture this. Mmm. Yes. Yes, I do believe the library will be on your left as you leave town. And you'll be goin' east. Or west. Or... whatever."

Jake shook his head, still squinting at the rain-obscured road ahead. Henrietta Penelope Barnwell had spoken the gospel truth when she'd confessed she wasn't very good with directions, he reflected. Hell, she'd probably have trouble telling someone which way was up!

He'd give this wild-goose chase five more minutes, he decided, glancing at the dashboard clock. It read 8:00 p.m. If he hadn't found the Barnwell place by then, he'd turn around and head to the Roadside Retreat Motel.

Jake didn't think of his current quest as looking for a place to live. All he required was a space to rest his head and stash his stuff for the next two months. To "live" in a place—to his mind, at least—implied making some kind of commitment. And Jake didn't do that. Oh, sure, he formed and fulfilled professional contracts. But that wasn't the same thing as making a commitment to a place... or a person. When it came to doing that, Jake Turner's standard answer was "Thanks, but no thanks."

The rain seemed to stop for a split second. Jake caught sight of something in the silvery glow of his truck's headlights that made him stomp on the brake. His pickup truck came to an abrupt halt. His body jerked forward, testing the restraint of his safety belt. After a moment, he settled back into his seat, staring out the rain-splattered window.

"Son of a . . ." Jake breathed, genuinely surprised.

There it was, on the left side of the road, just as Henrietta Penelope Barnwell had told him it would be: a white metal mailbox bearing the black-lettered name Barnwell. Amazing.

The mailbox sat atop a post that was planted next to a gravel driveway. Jake heard the crunch of small stones as he turned the truck onto the drive. Up ahead he saw a two-story, white clapboard house with a wraparound porch. Again, it was just as Henrietta Penelope Barnwell had told him it would be.

Jake stepped on the brakes, killed the engine and assessed the house with a professional eye. Despite the rain he was able to make out quite a few details. This was because every window on the first floor was lit up.

The place was about fifty years old, he decided after a few seconds, and it was in need of a lot of minor—maybe even some major—repair work. While it wasn't a ramshackle wreck by any means, it was a far cry from the exquisite antebellum mansion that had brought him to Deacon's Crossing.

And yet there was an aura of warmth about this particular house. No. *More* than that. There was an aura of *welcoming*. Maybe it was the way the windows glowed beckoningly through the gloom of the stormy night, but this house struck Jake as the kind of place a person could call home.

Not, he recognized, that he was an expert on the subject. *Home* was just another four-letter word to him. The closest he'd ever come to having a home was the over-the-garage apartment he leased from a curmudgeonly old woodworker named Sam Swayze.

Only one window on the second floor of the Barnwell house was lit. Jake's attention was drawn there by the sudden appearance of a silhouetted figure.

The figure was apparently nude and obviously female, although not overly endowed. Slim and supple were the adjectives that occurred to Jake. Slim and supple . . . like a willow.

She—whoever she was—stretched, slender arms reaching toward the ceiling. Jake tracked the languid elongation of her limbs. The sweet uplift of her small breasts. The elegant arch of her throat as she tilted her head back and her hair spilled away from her face. He shifted abruptly, his fingers fumbling at the buckle of his seat belt.

The buckle gave way with an audible click. Jake shifted again, conscious that the atmosphere in the cab of the truck had turned warm and close. Raindrops drummed on the metal roof above him. The noise they created seemed to merge with the pounding acceleration of his pulse.

The slender arms came down. The lithe body relaxed, posture returning to normal. After a second or two the figure moved gracefully away from the window.

Jake realized he'd been holding his breath. He released it with a soft hiss and averted his gaze from the rectangle of light on the second floor of the Barnwell house.

She couldn't be the old lady he'd spoken to on the phone, he told himself. No way, no how. Which meant she had to be the niece. Sally? Ally? No. *Callie.* The one who was running herself ragged trying to dress prom queens and Peanut Princesses.

Jake rubbed a hand over his chin, suddenly conscious that he was sporting nearly a week's worth of beard growth. He also became aware that forty-eight hours of wear had left his clothes less than fresh. His jeans had a splotch of grease on the upper right thigh where he'd wiped his hands after changing a tire about ten miles out of Baltimore the day before and his wash-faded black T-shirt bore traces of the chili dogs he'd wolfed down at a fast-food place in Atlanta just that morning.

He'd fleetingly considered sprucing himself up before he'd left Deacon's Crossing to look for the Barnwell place, but he'd discarded the idea for a number of reasons. He'd settled instead for a quick wash in the men's room of a filling station.

His decision to stay "as is" hadn't been prompted by any innate sloppiness. Nor was he out to offend people by flouting accepted standards of personal hygiene. He simply had no intention of pitching himself to anyone—landlady, client or lover—as something other than what he was.

Some folks considered him a master craftsman—even an artist. Jake had moments of fierce, flashing pride when he embraced both these characterizations. But he never forgot that most people, including his own mother, saw him as nothing but a manual laborer. After all, he possessed no high-tech skills, no college degree.

He could have appeared at the Barnwells' door wearing an immaculate suit and silk tie and smelling of deodorant, mouthwash and some expensive after-shave. He had all the necessary gear to effect such a transformation in the back of his truck. But to do that would have been misleading, because the "real" Jake Turner didn't spend his days spiffed up. The "real" Jake Turner spent his days working hard with his bare hands. And if Miss Henrietta Penelope Barnwell and her dear niece, Callie, turned their noses up at the way he looked tonight...

Jake's eyes strayed back to the lighted window on the second floor.

What you see is what you get, ladies, he thought with a trace of defiance. He reached for the door handle. Take it or leave it.

He covered the distance from the pickup to the porch in a dozen strides. Although his exposure to the rain lasted only a few seconds, it left his dark T-shirt clinging to his torso. He shook his head once or twice, then forked both hands through his moisture-spangled hair, slicking it straight back from his brow.

The floor of the porch creaked as Jake crossed it. The dash from the truck had left the running shoes he was wearing coated with orange-red Georgia mud. He scraped them against the mat set out in front of the door, then looked around for a bell to ring. There wasn't one. After a moment, he rapped his knuckles against the door and listened.

No response.

Jake knocked again. This time he heard a dog bark. The yip-yip-yapping was followed by the sound of a woman's voice. Although he couldn't make out the words, he had the impression the speaker was addressing the dog.

Eventually the door swung open to reveal a bonbon of a female who stood no more than five feet tall in her perfectly polished shoes. Her silvery-white hair was as fine as spun sugar and she was clad in a flouncy floral print dress that cried out for a ribbon-trimmed picture hat and a pair of spotless white gloves. She was the kind of little old lady any Boy Scout worth his merit badges would love to help cross a busy street.

"Oh, hush up, Buttercup," she was saying, wagging a plump finger at what had to be one of the sorriest-looking mutts Jake had ever seen. The word *mixed* didn't begin to describe the dog's breeding. The fact that the pooch was obviously expecting only added to its unprepossessing appearance. "Do you hear me? Just hush up!"

Amazingly the pregnant, pug-ugly animal did just that.

"Good dog," the woman crooned melodiously as Buttercup flopped down on the floor and subsided into ear-drooping, tongue-lolling silence.

"Miss Barnwell?" Jake questioned. "I'm Jake Tur—"

The final syllable died in his throat as the woman lifted her head to look at him. He saw the start of a charming smile. Then, without warning, the blood drained out of her dimpled cheeks. Jake watched as the woman's eyes grew huge and horrified.

"Harriman Gage?" she gasped. She clasped trembling hands to her ample and heaving bosom. "Oh, my God, *Harriman G-Ga-age!*"

The woman's voice soared and splintered on the last word. Her gaze clouded. Her body began to sway.

Prompted by an impulse he couldn't identify, Jake stepped through the open door and caught the woman as she keeled over in a faint. He grunted in surprise as she toppled against him. While the lady was small, she was as solid as an overstuffed chair.

The difference in their sizes made it difficult for him to get a decent grip on her. Jake was in the process of adjusting his hold when Buttercup suddenly gave a bloodcurdling yowl and reared up off the floor. An instant later, she hurled herself against him, nearly knocking him off his feet.

"Dammit!" he swore, desperately trying to maintain his balance. He stumbled, banging a shoulder against the still-open front door. "Dammit, dog! Sit! *Sit!* No! Buttercu— no! Don't do—"

But Buttercup did. Barking wildly, the mongrel mother-to-be launched an all-out assault on Jake's left leg. Teeth. Paws. Teeth. Paws. Jake grimaced when he heard the sound of ripping denim. He winced when he felt the rake of a canine incisor.

Jake swore again. Loudly.

There seemed to be just three options open to him. Unfortunately none was acceptable under his code of behavior.

There was no way he could dump an unconscious little old lady on her keister—no matter how well-upholstered that keister happened to be.

Nor was there any way he could kick a pregnant pooch— not even if the pooch in question seemed bent on reducing his favorite pair of jeans to shreds.

And as for opening his mouth and hollering for help—

"F-freeze, you son of a b-bitch!"

The source of this shaky order was a shotgun-toting teenager standing about ten feet away. Jake had absolutely no idea where he'd materialized from. That the kid was scared was obvious. His tension-pleated brow was sheened with perspiration and his prominent Adam's apple bobbed furiously in his throat. But underneath the fear there was determination. A chill of apprehension shivered its way up

Jake's spine. He felt the fine hairs on the back of his neck come to attention.

The youth advanced three steps. While there was an adolescent gawkiness to his movements, his expression was grimly adult.

"Look, kid," Jake began, striving for a calm, quiet tone. "I know how this must look, but—"

Without warning, the woman he was still clutching began to stir. "Oooooo," she moaned.

The barrel of the shotgun wavered and ended up aimed at what Jake considered a particularly vital portion of his anatomy.

"Aunt H-Henny?" the boy asked, his voice cracking. The grown-up gravity of just a few seconds before vanished from his freckle-spattered face, leaving him looking very young and vulnerable.

The woman who'd been addressed as Aunt Henny moaned again and started to flail her arms.

"Let go of her, you bastard!" the boy shouted, brandishing his weapon.

"Kid, believe me, there's nothing I'd like—oomph!"

Jake sucked in his breath sharply as he took an elbow in the solar plexus. The little old lady packed quite a punch! He staggered a half step to the left, stumbling over Buttercup. The pooch let out an ungodly howl of indignation and bolted.

Jake saw the boy lunge for him, shotgun still in hand. He also saw the boy trip—apparently over the damned dog— and start to fall forward. Somehow Jake managed to slam the barrel of the weapon upward with the flat of one hand without dropping his squirming, silver-haired burden.

Ka-blam!

The weapon hit the floor.

So did the teenager.

And the mutt.

The old lady would have wound up on the floor, too, if Jake hadn't tightened his grip on her.

A blizzard of plaster chips and dust descended from the ceiling.

Everything went very still. Very silent.

And then Jake lifted his eyes and saw her. She was standing on the staircase at the far end of the entrance hall. A slender woman with a wavy cloud of cinnamon brown hair, she was clad in an oversized scarlet T-shirt that stopped about three inches shy of her well-shaped knees.

He watched her scan the scene before her, apparently searching for casualties and assessing damage. The expression on her face changed from acute anxiety to obvious exasperation. Finally, in a movement that lifted the bottom of her T-shirt to tantalizing new heights, she planted her hands on her hips.

"Just what in the name of the Lord is going on down here?" she demanded in a voice that was half smoke, half honey.

Every masculine instinct Jake had told him that *this* was the woman whose silhouette he'd seen in the second-floor window.

Two

"There, there, Aunt Henny," Caroline "Callie" Barnwell said soothingly about fifteen minutes later. "There, there."

She patted her aunt's plump shoulder, wordlessly urging her to drink the fine old sherry she'd poured for her. Callie knew that while Henrietta Penelope Barnwell proclaimed herself a teetotaler, she was prone to taking a nip on occasion to settle her nerves. And if ever nerves needed settling, it was now!

Callie had been called on to sort out a lot of sticky situations since she'd assumed charge of her family at age twenty-four. But none of the tribulations she'd endured during the previous six years had prepared her to handle Jake Turner's chaotic entrance into her home and life.

Callie figured she'd be dead and buried before she forgot her first glimpse of the tawny-haired, powerfully built Northerner who was now sitting in a ladder-backed chair not five feet from her. It wasn't simply that the situation in which she'd initially encountered him was so memorable, although there was no disputing that the plaster-dusted tableau she'd discovered in the front hallway was one for the books. No, it was more a matter of having known, instantly and absolutely, that she'd just caught sight of a man who was going to have a profound impact on her—whether she liked it or not.

The certainty she'd felt about this had been—and still was—unnerving, almost frightening. Callie prided herself on being a lot of things, but prescient wasn't one of them. After all, she hadn't had the faintest inkling about the future when she'd met Mark Stephens eight years before and *he'd* ended up breaking her heart. But the instant she'd laid eyes on the man who'd eventually introduced himself as Jake Turner, every fiber of her brain and body had responded.

Callie couldn't explain her reaction. If she had a "type"—and she wasn't at all sure she did—tall, tanned and tough wasn't it. Yet those adjectives pretty much summed up the man who'd caused her sixty-seven-year-old aunt to swoon and her sixteen-year-old half brother to shoot a hole in the hallway ceiling.

Tall.

Tanned.

Tough.

And possessed of the most vivid pair of blue-green eyes Callie had seen. Eyes which were studying her with laser-like intensity at this very instant.

This scrutiny was unsettling to Callie for a great many reasons, including that her hair was uncombed, her face was unmade-up and her sole piece of attire was a four-year-old, extra-large T-shirt. But at the top of the list of reasons was the distinct impression that Jake's response to her was just as potent as hers to him. She couldn't articulate why she'd formed this impression; it wasn't based on anything specific the man had said or done. Yet she had the unshakable feeling that in the same split second she'd looked at Jake Turner and seen destiny, he'd looked at her and seen . . .

Well, she wasn't certain *what* he'd seen—or was now seeing. Impending disaster, maybe. But whatever it was, she sensed it made him extremely uneasy.

Henny took a gulp of her sherry, then picked a few small fragments of plaster off the skirt of her dress. "I feel so foolish, Callie," she declared plaintively. "It's just that when I opened the door and saw Mr. Turner standin' there..." Her voice trailed off and she took another drink.

"It was dark and you were taken by surprise," Callie said comfortingly. She was unable to prevent herself from glancing at Jake. Their eyes met for an instant.

Callie sank into the love seat next to her aunt, feeling a little light-headed. She cleared her throat, then added, "I'm sure Mr. Turner understands."

"Oh, absolutely, Miss Barnwell," Jake answered in an uninflected voice, forcing himself to shift his gaze from Callie to her aunt. He understood that Henrietta Penelope Barnwell had briefly mistaken him for someone named Harriman Gage. Exactly who this guy was and what he'd done, Jake didn't know. But he thought he could make a pretty shrewd guess based on the way the little old lady was soaking up the sherry.

And as for the guesses he could make based on the way her niece was checking him out with those clear hazel eyes...

Callie Barnwell didn't like him, that much was obvious. What was not so obvious was why he should give a damn about her dislike. She wasn't his type. Oh, all right, maybe there was a part of him that wanted to see in the skin what he'd glimpsed in silhouette earlier. And maybe there was another part of him that wouldn't mind finding out whether her mouth tasted as good as it looked. But she *still* wasn't his type. In fact, she was about as far from his type as a female could get.

This was because physical attributes weren't all that important when it came to determining whether a woman was or wasn't his type. Jake wasn't hung up on hair color or height or bra cup size. For him, the clincher was personality.

Personality as in character.

Personality as in basic, bottom-line nature.

To put it bluntly: Jake Turner had always limited his involvements—if *involvements* was the right word for his string of no-string affairs—to women who had as little desire for long-term entanglements as he did.

Instinct warned him that it would be a cold day in hell before the spunky Miss Caroline Barnwell came anywhere near falling into this category. She was the kind of woman who'd complicate a man's life whether he wanted her to or not. What's more, she'd very likely do it without trying and probably without even being aware of what was going on.

All she'd have to do was to be herself.

In short it shouldn't have been any skin off Jake Turner's nose if Henrietta Penelope Barnwell's intriguing-looking niece hated his guts. Nonetheless, the hostility he sensed emanating from Callie irritated him. Like an itch he couldn't scratch, it was irritating him more with each passing moment.

Jake didn't expect every female he met to fall at his feet or fawn over him. While he tended to have more than his share of luck with the ladies, he understood that a man couldn't score one hundred percent of the time. But, dammit, he'd never had a woman examine him the way Callie Barnwell was. What the hell was she thinking, anyway?

Callie hadn't intended to stare at Jake. But once she'd started looking at him, it was impossible not to mentally compare his lean, compelling face to the one depicted in the faded pencil sketch that was a key reminder of the most infamous episode in her family's history.

There was a definite visual kinship between the two emphatically male faces, she decided after an uncomfortable moment of contemplation. Enough that her aunt's characteristically melodramatic reaction couldn't be written off as totally irrational. This kinship was as much a matter of overall expression as individual features. Both Harriman Gage and Jake Turner looked like very independent—some might say arrogant—men. They projected the same aura.

There was one striking similarity in terms of their individual features, too. Both men had a distinctly sensual set to their lips. And while Callie thought it unlikely that her dear and ditsy relative had registered this particular fact, she herself couldn't overlook it.

Then again, perhaps she was underestimating her aunt's level of womanly awareness. After all, she never would have believed that the ancestress after whom she'd been named would've paid much attention to the shape of a man's mouth, either, if she hadn't had handwritten proof of the fact.

I fear I am being led into temptation by Mr. Harriman Gage's lips, Caroline Anne Barnwell had confided to her personal journal on June 3, 1874. *Each time we meet, I find myself gazing at his mouth and experiencing the most disturbing sensations in areas too intimate to name even here. I am certain these sensations are wicked. Or, at the very least, unladylike. And yet...*

Callie broke off her silent recitation of this diary passage—one of dozens she knew by heart. Her abrupt return to the present was prompted by the realization that she'd been looking at Jake Turner for an embarrassingly long period of time. She felt herself start to flush. The heat in her cheeks intensified when she became aware of the fact that her aunt had been speaking to her and she hadn't registered a word of what had been said.

"I'm sorry, Aunt Henny," she apologized, tearing her eyes away from Jake's face. "I'm afraid I wasn't listening."

What is wrong with me? Callie wondered. Yes, an unusually trying day at the dress shop had thrown her off balance and yes, the insane scene in the hallway had undermined what little equilibrium she'd had left. But neither of these circumstances explained why she should feel so vulnerable to a man she'd met barely a quarter of an hour before!

She was willing to acknowledge that Jake Turner was attractive in a disreputable, dangerous kind of way. The beard growth that shadowed his cheeks and jaw and the shaggy hair that curled over his nape and ears seemed to enhance the angular sensuality of his rugged features rather than detract from it. And there was no denying—if she wanted to get downright crude about it—that Jake Turner filled out his snug-fitting jeans better than anyone she'd ever run into. It was obvious he was all male, all muscle.

She also had to concede that the man had demonstrated courage under fire out in the front hallway. More than a few members of his sex would have turned tail and run in the same situation. He, however, had stayed cool and stood his ground.

But, even so . . .

"All I was sayin', Callie dear," her aunt declared sweetly, "is that I'm relieved to know Mr. Turner's profession requires him to keep up to date with his tetanus shots. Workin' with nails and all, he can't avoid getting stuck with somethin' rusty every now and again, so he has to take precautions. It's not that I think my precious Buttercup might be carryin' lockjaw germs—or the germs of any other disease, for that matter. In my opinion, the only thing Buttercup's carryin' is *puppies*. Still, I've heard just awful stories about folks dyin' long and terrible deaths after gettin' bit by a dog. So it sets my mind at ease to know that Mr. Turner's medically protected. I'm sure it soothes you, too."

"Oh, of course, Aunt Henny," Callie concurred with less than complete sincerity.

"I'm sure it soothes you as well, Mr. Turner," Henny went on. She drained the remainder of her sherry and set down the glass.

"It certainly does, ma'am," he agreed, then glanced briefly at Callie. There was an odd sparkle in her wide, gray-green eyes and a quirky set to her rather stubborn jaw. Damned if he didn't get the feeling that she was getting a perverse kick from the idea of his contracting some kind of illness!

"Now, you're certain you don't want Callie to tend to your injuries?" Henny inquired, nodding her silver-haired head at the appropriate portion of Jake's anatomy. The left leg of his jeans had been reduced to rags from the knee downward. The shin and well-muscled calf visible through the shredded denim bore a number of scratches and teeth marks. "She's got a delicate touch."

Yeah, Jake reflected sardonically, he'd just bet she did. If the provocative expression on Callie's face was anything to judge by, she'd probably like to use her "delicate" touch to deprive him of one or two body parts! Of course, it *might* be worth running the risk just to experience the feel of the lady's slender-fingered hands—

Jake slammed the door on this particular line of thought. Was he losing his mind? he wondered. What in the name of heaven was he doing spinning a sexual fantasy about a woman he could never have? A woman he wouldn't want even if he *could* have her! Dreaming about Callie Barnwell was going to get him nothing but trouble and he knew it.

"Mr. Turner?" Henny prompted.

"Uh, yes...ma'am?" he returned. Just why were these Barnwell women getting to him so badly? he asked himself, shifting in his seat. The aunt made him remember manners he hadn't realized he'd learned. The niece made him want to forget the few tenets of gentlemanly behavior he'd ever stuck to.

"I was inquirin' if you might want to reconsider Callie's offer to tend to your leg," the older woman said. If she was conscious of the disjointed nature of this conversation, she gave no indication of it.

"Aunt Henny—" Callie started. In point of fact, the offer of tending had been made by her relative, not her. The last thing she wanted to do was touch Jake Turner! It wasn't that she thought physical contact with the man would be unpleasant. Just very...*very*...unwise.

"Ah, no." Jake shook his head and glanced downward. Although the left leg of his jeans had been badly torn, the flesh beneath was intact. There was no blood. Indeed, despite the frenzied nature of her attack, Buttercup had only broken his skin in one spot. "No, thank you, ma'am. I'm just fine."

The older woman accepted this rebuff serenely. "I'm certain you know best, Mr. Turner. But you *must* let us do somethin' about your poor jeans. Why, it just humiliates me no end to see how Buttercup ravaged your clothing. Still, as bad as it looks, I'm absolutely positive my niece can have you stitched back up in no time."

Oh, no, thought Callie, stiffening with alarm. Aunt Henny's not actually going to suggest—

"All you have to do is take off—"

Oh, dear Lord, she was!

Callie opened her mouth to prevent her aunt from finishing this sentence. She was forestalled by the sudden reappearance of her half brother.

"I finally got Buttercup settled down out on the back porch," he announced without preamble. His voice was a note or two higher than usual and he was focusing exclusively on his aunt. "She seems all right, Aunt Henny."

"Oh, bless you, P.D.," the older woman responded, placing one hand over her heart. "I'm so relieved."

There was an awkward pause.

Palmer Dean Barnwell the Third exuded uneasiness from the top of his plaster-flecked, brown-haired head to the tips of his filthy bare feet. His face was pale, his hands were clenched, and the set of his shoulders and spine was rigid.

Callie saw her half brother's gaze cut to Jake Turner for an instant, then dart away. He looked around the room until he spotted the shotgun she'd retrieved earlier and propped against the wall until she could lock it up. Hot, humiliated color rushed into his cheeks. She noted that he completely avoided looking at her.

Poor kid, Jake thought, experiencing an unexpected flash of sympathy. It was obvious the boy had the shakes about confronting him. But that was understandable. Who wouldn't be shaken by the prospect of coming face to face with somebody they'd nearly shot?

What interested Jake was P.D.'s attitude toward Callie. She, clearly, was the authority figure in this household. That had to be rough on the boy—and on her. Jake remembered his own troubled adolescence well enough to deduce that the kid was going through a stage when rules were good for nothing but breaking. If those rules were being laid down by a half sister who couldn't be more than twenty-nine or thirty...

Yeah, he concluded. It had to be real rough on both of them.

"Well, don't take root there in the doorway, P.D.," Henny said after several long moments. "Come in and meet our guest. Even in these unmannerly times, I don't believe that threatenin' a man with a shotgun constitutes a proper introduction."

Jake rose to his feet as the teenager approached him. He wasn't certain why, it just felt like the right thing to do.

P.D. was a few inches shorter than Jake and many pounds lighter. He moved as though his height had been acquired recently and he wasn't quite accustomed to it.

"Palmer Dean Barnwell the Third," he announced, sticking out his right hand.

Jake clasped the proffered hand and shook it. He liked how the kid didn't try to turn the contact into a squeezing contest. P.D. had a nice, firm grip, but he didn't press it, which was just as well. Jake had enough strength in his own fingers to crack walnuts.

"Jake Turner," he responded evenly. "The one and only."

The handshake ended. Jake saw one corner of P.D.'s mouth begin to turn up for a second. Then the teenager's expression grew wary once again.

"Mr. Turner, I'm sorry about what happened in the hall-way," he said feelingly. "*Real* sorry."

"The name's Jake and there's no need to apologize." A small portion of Jake's mind noted that P.D.'s drawl was much more marked than Callie's. He wondered whether she'd made a deliberate effort to shed her Southern accent.

"But—"

Jake aborted P.D.'s protest with a gesture. "You were protecting your family, kid," he said. "I admire that."

"You—you *do?*"

The kid was desperate for approval, Jake realized with a shock. More specifically, he was desperate for *male* approval. Being praised for protecting his family had obviously nourished a deep need in him.

Jake was surprised to discover he relished the idea that something he'd said had had such a positive effect on somebody. He wasn't completely comfortable with the notion, but he liked it nonetheless.

"Absolutely, P.D.," he answered solemnly, feeling an odd sense of satisfaction when he saw the teenager's skinny chest puff out. He then shifted into a cowboy cadence. "After all, a man's gotta do what a man's gotta do—right?"

Callie had been watching this exchange with a mounting sense of disbelief. What was going on here? she asked herself. Instead of accepting P.D.'s apology as any sane individual would do, Jake Turner was behaving as though the episode in the hallway had been some kind of male bonding ritual! And her half brother, Lord love him, was lapping it all up—including Jake Turner's atrocious imitation of John Wayne.

Callie tossed a quick look to her left, hoping to draw support from her aunt. Rather than appearing upset by what was happening, Henrietta Penelope Barnwell was beaming at P.D. and Jake.

Callie suppressed a groan, squared her shoulders and cleared her throat. It was up to her. All right. Fine. She'd coped with far greater problems than Mr. Jake Turner in the six years since she'd received a telephone call telling her that a car accident had left her stepmother dead and her father in critical condition. Compared to some of the challenges she'd faced and overcome, dealing with this man was going to be a piece of cake!

"I hadn't realized that a man was required to blast a hole in the ceiling of his family's home to prove his masculinity, Mr. Turner," she said very clearly.

Her comment didn't seem to faze Jake one bit. It did, however, prompt P.D. to look at her.

Well, no, he didn't really look *at* her. What he did was to turn his head in her general direction, roll his eyes and declare a bit belligerently, "I didn't know the gun was loaded, Callie."

Although her relationship with her half brother had been less than smooth in recent months, Callie wasn't accustomed to being sassed by him. "I'm sure Mr. Turner would have taken great comfort in that, if you'd blown his head off, P.D.," she snapped.

Jake decided it was time to run a little interference for the kid.

"Well, actually, Miss Barnwell," he interpolated dryly, "it wasn't my *head* I was worried about losing." When P.D.'s eyes snapped back to his, he gave the teenager a man-to-man wink. Damned if the kid didn't snicker and give him a wink in return.

Jake glanced at Callie. Her cheeks were flushed, her eyes were flashing. She looked furious.

Good, he thought. Somehow, some way, this woman had gotten under his skin. He intended to repay the favor with interest.

Callie forced herself to swallow several extremely cutting remarks. Her restraint wasn't simply a matter of adhering to the rules of ladylike behavior that had been drummed into her skull when she was a little girl. No, the main reason she kept quiet was that she knew Jake Turner was baiting her. It was plain as the stripes on a skunk that he wanted to make her lose her temper.

Well, she wasn't going to give him the satisfaction of having that happen. In fact, she wasn't going to give him any satisfaction at all!

"Why don't you...men...sit down?" Callie inquired in a sugary tone after several seconds. Crossing her legs ever so properly at the ankles, she carefully tugged the hem of her T-shirt down as far as it would go, then folded her hands primly in her lap. She proceeded to gaze limpidly at her half brother and his macho new mentor.

Jake cocked one tawny brow, acknowledging her self-control.

"Thank you," he responded and did as she'd suggested. After a moment, P.D. followed suit.

"So, Mr. Turner," Henny piped up pleasantly, "are you still thinkin' about rentin' a room from us?"

Jake was surprised into grinning. He really had to hand it to this little old lady. He couldn't tell whether she was genuinely scatterbrained or just putting on an act. But whichever she was, she plainly had no qualms about trying to breathe new life into subjects most other folks would rate ready for burial.

"Yes, ma'am, Miss Barnwell," he answered. "I am."

It was strange how those *ma'am*s kept on rolling off his tongue. Still, despite the strangeness, it felt right to address Henrietta Penelope Barnwell in a respectful manner. It felt right in the same way it had felt right to give young Palmer Dean the Third's obviously shaky male ego a boost.

"Good. Good. I'm so glad." The older woman nodded happily. "Now, I don't believe you mentioned how long you intend to stay on?"

"About two months."

"Till the end of August?"

"Yes, ma'am."

"My, that is a shame. If you leave at the end of August, you'll miss our annual Founders' Day Festival."

The mention of the festival rang a bell. "That's the event your niece is doing the costumes for?"

"Gowns, Mr. Turner," Callie corrected sharply. "In addition to owning a dress shop, I design and make *gowns* for special occasions."

"Last year's third runner-up in the Miss All-American Beauty of Georgia pageant wore one of Callie's creations," P.D. volunteered proudly. He leaned forward a little when

Jake turned his way. "'Course, she went and told a whole lot of folks she would've finished higher if Callie'd cut her gown lower so she could've shown off more of her baz—"

"P.D.!"

The teenager shifted his attention to his half sister. "What?" he asked, clearly taken aback by her tone.

"There is no need for you to bore Mr. Turner by repeating confidential comments," Callie informed him through gritted teeth.

Callie was certain that their would-be boarder was finding this conversation very funny. Even if he wasn't laughing on the outside, he undoubtedly was whooping it up on the inside. Well, Jake Turner could choke on his chuckles for all she cared. The gown-making part of her business helped keep her aunt and half brother fed, clothed and sheltered. True, running a small shop in Deacon's Crossing was a far cry from the dreams of Seventh Avenue success she'd once cherished. But, dammit, she'd done all right.

"Confidential?" P.D. repeated dubiously. "Callie, there's nothin' confidential when it comes to how Janie Mae Winslow feels about her bazooms. Heck, half the county must have heard her hollering when she lost—"

"Now, Palmer Dean," Henny interrupted gently. "There's no need to rake up old muck."

"Janie Mae Winslow," Jake echoed. "Is she the one who wants to be the, ah, Peanut Princess?"

Henrietta Barnwell smiled at him. "Why, that's absolutely right! How ever did you know?"

"You said something about it when we spoke on the phone."

"Did I?" The older woman frowned. "Mmm, now that you mention it, I *do* seem to recollect...but fancy you rememberin' a detail like that!"

Jake glanced at Callie. He had the sense he'd stung her professional pride. This bothered him. It was one thing to ruffle the lady's feathers, entirely another to cause her to think he had no respect for the way she earned her living.

Jake didn't demean other people's work, be it digging a ditch or developing a cure for cancer.

"You're making Janie Mae Winslow's—ah—gown for the contest, aren't you, Miss Barnwell?" he questioned. "For the Peanut thing, I mean."

Callie fluffed her hair with her fingers. She didn't know how to interpret the expression in Jake's blue-green eyes. It seemed almost apologetic.

"Yes, Mr. Turner," she replied warily. "I am."

"Well, then, no matter what she tells people, Janie Mae must think you're very good at what you do. And that's what counts. Clients can complain all they want, but if they keep coming back for more..." He cocked a brow significantly.

This has to be a trick, Callie thought uneasily. This interloper was trying to fool her into thinking he was capable of being nice. But if she fell for his act, heaven only knew what kind of advantage he'd take! He'd probably stomp over her the way Sherman had stomped over Georgia, if she gave him half a chance.

Lord, she was going to have to be on her guard every single solitary second of the next two months if he rented the room upstairs!

"I pride myself on doing what's best for my customers," she said.

There was a brief pause.

"So, what exactly are you doin' here in Deacon's Crossing, Mr. Turner?" P.D. asked after a moment.

"Jake," Jake corrected, turning toward the teenager.

The kid's eyes flicked toward his half sister, then back to Jake's face. "Jake," he repeated.

"Mr. Turner's in town to restore somethin', P.D.," Henny declared.

"That's right," Jake affirmed. "I'm a carpenter. I'm going to be doing custom work on a place not too far from here. You must know it. It's called Belle Terre."

It seemed to Jake that the temperature in the room suddenly plummeted. The silence that descended on the parlor could only be described as chilly.

"Quarter Oaks," P.D. said finally.

"What?" Jake asked, confused.

"It's called Quarter Oaks," the teenager elaborated. "There're twenty-five oak trees on the property."

"But—"

"Some people refer to it as Belle Terre, Mr. Turner," Callie interrupted, her tone making it abundantly clear what she thought of those particular people. "But its true name is Quarter Oaks."

"I see," Jake replied, not at all sure that he did.

"Quarter Oaks was our family home for many, many years," Henny said. "Unfortunately it was lost to us after the Late Unpleasantness."

The Late Unpleasantness? Jake repeated silently. What the hell was the Late—

"Are you—are you talking about the Civil War?" he asked tentatively.

The atmosphere in the parlor became absolutely Arctic.

"In this household, Mr. Turner, we prefer the phrase The War for Southern Independence," Henrietta Penelope Barnwell informed him in a voice that was hard enough to cut glass.

The sudden transformation from sweet little old lady to stainless steel magnolia stunned Jake. He'd heard that some Southerners were still touchy about the Civil—er, the War for Southern Independence. But he'd had no idea the sensitivity ran this deep. Short of standing up and whistling "Dixie", he didn't think there was a lot he could do to persuade Henrietta Barnwell he hadn't meant to offend.

"Ah . . . yes, ma'am," he said finally.

Henny's stiffened features softened into a charming smile. "I'm so glad you understand," she replied. "Now, I'm sure you'd like to take a look at the room we're offerin'. Callie dear, why don't you escort Mr. Turner upstairs and show him what he wants to see?"

Although he knew this last suggestion was made in a spirit of utter innocence, Jake felt his body start to stir. The words *upstairs* and *see* inevitably made him think of the slender feminine silhouette he'd glimpsed in one of the Barnwell's second-floor windows.

God, he thought, rubbing his palms against the sides of his denim-clad thighs. Did he *really* want to spend the next two months in the same house as Callie Barnwell?

"Mr. Turner?" Callie prompted, getting to her feet. She couldn't help but wonder why he'd flushed so suddenly. Jake Turner hadn't struck her as a man with an ounce of shame to his name.

Jake looked at Callie. Yeah, he conceded to himself. As crazy as he realized it was, he really did want to spend the next two months in the same house as Callie Barnwell.

"Mr. Turner?" Callie repeated, experiencing an odd fluttering in the pit of her stomach.

"I'm right with you."

The room was fine. It was larger than Jake had expected and pleasantly done up in shades of blue and ivory. The furniture—including a king-sized bed and polished oak armoire—had a solidly masculine look.

"I'll take it," he said.

He and Callie quickly came to terms, although he got the distinct feeling she wasn't pleased when he announced he'd like to move in that very night.

"I'll have P.D. help bring in your things," she told him after a brief but eloquent hesitation. "And I'll take care of changing the sheets on the bed."

"Thanks."

"You're welcome," she returned politely, then started to turn away.

"Callie—" Prompted by an urge he didn't want to examine too closely, Jake reached out and caught her arm.

Callie pivoted back to face him. A tinge of peachy pink stained the fine-grained skin of her cheeks. She shrugged free of his grasp and lifted her chin.

"Yes, Mr. Turner?"

She wasn't beautiful. She wasn't "built." But, Lord, there was something about Callie Barnwell that reached right to the marrow with Jake. He wanted to sift the strands of her wavy hair through his fingers and catalogue all the different shades of brown they included. He wanted to gaze into her long-lashed eyes and count every single one of the colors encompassed in their changeable hazel depths. He wanted—

"Did you want somethin' else, Mr. Turner?" Her drawl was suddenly very evident.

Jake blinked and jammed his hands in his pockets. A series of disjointed questions skipped across the surface of his mind like stones across a pond. The one that ultimately popped out of his mouth was pretty much a matter of chance.

"Just who in hell is Harriman Gage?" he asked.

Callie's chin went up another notch. Her answer, when it came, was as dulcet and Dixie-fied as fresh peach preserves.

"Harriman Gage," she said, "was the no-good, low-down Yankee who ruined my great-great-great-great-aunt, Caroline Anne."

Three

One week later Callie stood in the kitchen of the Barnwell house sorting through a huge mound of dirty laundry. Her movements were rhythmic and ruthless. Light things had to be separated from dark ones. Items requiring delicate handling needed to be winnowed out from the wash-and-wear.

Socks.

A lace-trimmed slip and an embroidered blouse.

One...two...three...four T-shirts.

Two bras.

Another blouse, this one white with pin tucks.

A pair of—

Callie flung the skimpy piece of clothing she'd just picked up away from her.

Black cotton briefs. Very *brief* black cotton briefs that definitely did not belong to her half brother, P.D.

Lord, wasn't that just what she should have expected from Jake Turner? Callie asked herself.

Actually it was a wonder the man was able to wear underwear at all! Those jeans he strutted around in looked as though they'd been laminated on. It was a miracle he could bend over or sit down in them, much less get another layer of material beneath.

"Damn the man," Callie muttered to herself.

It hadn't been her idea to do Jake Turner's laundry. Doing his laundry was not part of the original deal. No, the idea of offering to do Jake's laundry had originated with her darling, deluded aunt. And once the offer had been made and accepted, there'd been no graceful way for Callie to renege on the arrangement.

Sheets.

A floral print shirtwaist dress.

A trio of towels that looked as though they'd been used to mop the floor of a garage.

Two more pairs of men's cotton briefs. White this time.

Callie ground her teeth and kept on sorting. She had an hour and fifteen minutes to do laundry, then she had to go to her shop. Saturday was always a busy day at Callie's Corner and she needed to make certain everything was ready for her customers. She could not afford to be distracted.

She would have bet biscuits to buckshot that Jake Turner couldn't possibly have turned things any more topsy-turvy than he had the night he'd arrived. But she would have lost the wager. In seven short days, he'd thoroughly upset the ordered life it had taken her six long years to establish.

Two sleeveless knit pullovers. One sky blue, the other mint green.

A mud-stained pair of jeans. Definitely P.D.'s.

Callie methodically turned the pockets of the filthy denim garment inside out. She recovered forty-seven cents in change, the nub of a pencil and a wadded up wrapper from a chocolate bar.

Of course, none of the other members of her family saw anything to fault in Jake Turner, Callie reflected sourly. Oh, no. *They* thought he was so wonderful, they were ready to eat him up with a spoon.

Callie grimaced.

All right. She was willing to acknowledge that the man wasn't completely devoid of redeeming features. After all, he *had* replastered the hole in the hallway ceiling. He'd also taken it upon himself to do some repair work on the front porch. He'd even managed to pry open a pair of upstairs windows that had been painted shut before she'd been born.

Even so, it was Callie's considered opinion—and, heaven knew, she'd spent a lot of time considering this subject—that Jake Turner was trouble with a capital *T*. It made no difference to her that he could apparently hit a nail on the head every time he swung a hammer. The man had cast a spell on her aunt and half brother, and she intended to break it even if she had to use dynamite to do it!

Aunt Henny doted on their new tenant. She insisted on calling him Jacob and made a fluttery fuss every time he walked into the house. P.D. was even worse. *He'd* turned the man into a role model! Of all the people in the world to pick as an idol, he'd chosen a shaggy-haired thirty-five-year-old with no apparent roots or family.

Callie would swear until her dying day that she'd seen her half brother's limited supply of good sense drain right out of his head when he'd discovered that one of the things Jake Turner was transporting in the back of his pickup was a motorcycle. A big, black *monster* of a motorcycle. And when Jake had actually allowed him to ride the thing, it had been obvious that P.D. had thought he'd expired and gone to heaven!

Callie yanked another pair of the teenager's jeans out of the heap of laundry. This pair was in immaculate condition compared with the previous one. Sighing heavily, she began the process of searching through the pockets. She never knew what she was going to find in her half brother's clothing.

Of course, she mused unhappily, the coup de grace was that even Buttercup had become Jake Turner's devoted follower. Yes, indeed. The same dog who had tried to tear the Yankee's leg off now slept on the end of his bed and slavered over his feet! It was enough to make a person—

"Oh... my... God..." Callie gasped, suddenly realizing what she'd just extracted from P.D.'s jeans. Too shocked to say anything else, she simply stared at the small, foil-wrapped object she held in the palm of her shaking right hand.

Jake descended from the second floor of the Barnwell house with his latest bed partner in his arms. He moved quietly. Because the doors to their bedrooms had been closed when he'd gone by them, he assumed both Miss Henny and P.D. were still asleep. He had no intention of waking either of them.

Jake didn't mind lugging Buttercup up and down the stairs. He'd hauled heavier burdens in his time. Besides, carrying the poor pregnant mutt was definitely preferable to watching her struggle with the steps. The only thing he objected to was the way she licked his face whenever he picked her up.

"Okay, Buttercup," he said once he'd reached the bottom of the staircase. He hunkered down and set the pooch on the floor. "This is the end of the line."

He straightened, then used the back of one hand to wipe the dog slobber off his face. His clean-shaven skin felt as though it had been scoured by Buttercup's sandpapery tongue.

The dog whimpered for attention and started lapping at the battered work shoes Jake was wearing. Although he liked going barefoot, Jake had decided he'd better forgo the pleasure as long as he was residing in the Barnwell house. Not only did he have an aversion to walking on dog drool, but he was also extremely ticklish around the toes.

"That's enough of that," he said, gently nudging the animal. Buttercup backed off a little, gazing up at him with inquiring eyes. Her stubby tail wagged back and forth like a metronome.

Jake glanced at his watch. Nearly seven-thirty. He planned to head to the site about eight. There was no hurry.

It was Saturday, after all. The contract he'd signed was for Mondays through Fridays. Still, there was some finishing work he wanted to get done, and he saw no reason to put it off.

He figured the job would take four, maybe five hours. After that—who knew?

Maybe he'd come back and let P.D. take another spin on his Harley. Or maybe he'd come back and do a little tinkering around the house. Then again, maybe he'd cruise into Deacon's Crossing and whisk Callie away from her dress shop for an intimate afternoon interlude at the Roadside Retreat Motel.

Jake snorted. Oh, sure. About the only way he'd ever get Miss Caroline Barnwell to go anywhere with him—much less to a motel—would be to tie her up and take her there by force. He'd have to gag her, too. The lady had a tongue like a table saw when she got angry. And he'd need to throw on a blindfold as well, because she could say almost as much with her eyes as she could with her mouth.

Jake forked his fingers back through his hair, then shook his head. Callie really, truly aggravated him. And the fact that she really, truly aggravated him aggravated him even more.

He'd told himself at least a dozen times a day to stop thinking about her. He'd reminded himself that she wasn't his type, but images of her kept sneaking into his mind and sliding into his dreams.

Callie brought out something that no other woman ever had. Whether this something was the best or worst in him, Jake couldn't tell. He only knew he couldn't maintain his cool around her. He felt a constant need to push her...provoke her...make her acknowledge him, even if that acknowledgment involved nothing more than a gray-green glance of disapproval.

Hell. Maybe he was just intent on living down to the low opinion she'd obviously formed of him the first night they'd met. There'd been a time when he'd been prone to that kind of behavior. Could be he was suffering a relapse of—

Jake broke off, frowning, as he heard an odd noise. It sounded as though it had come from the kitchen. Stepping carefully over Buttercup's ungainly body, he headed in that direction.

"Callie?" he questioned softly as he pushed open the kitchen door.

She was standing in the middle of the room, surrounded by piles of laundry. She was clutching a pair of blue jeans in her left hand and a small object he couldn't immediately identify in her right. The expression on her face was a vivid mix of shocked dismay and stunned disbelief. She seemed to be unaware that someone had spoken to her.

"Callie?" Jake repeated, raising his voice and sharpening his tone. He stepped into the kitchen. The door swung creakily shut behind him. The sound of toenails scrabbling against linoleum told him that Buttercup was dogging his footsteps.

He saw Callie start, then register his presence. Her fingers opened. The jeans and whatever she'd been holding fell to the floor.

Jake crossed to her in three quick strides, then bent to retrieve the items she'd dropped.

"I—" she croaked, apparently protesting his action.

Jake understood everything the instant he got a good look at the object Callie had had in her right hand. A perverse impulse grabbed him the instant after that. Knowing he'd probably regret doing so, he gave into it without a fight.

"Getting ready for a hot date?" he inquired as he straightened.

"Wh-what?" Callie asked.

Jake displayed the foil-covered condom he'd picked up. "Hot date?" he repeated meaningfully.

He saw Callie realize what he was implying. A rush of hot color stained her cheeks and her eyes went green with temper. A split second after she'd made the connection, she snatched the prophylactic away from him.

"Don't be crude!" she snapped angrily, stuffing the condom into the pocket of the trim blue cotton skirt she was wearing.

"Crude?" Jake feigned hurt. "I was being complimentary."

"Complimentary?"

"Sure. Some women seem to think that passion and protection don't mix. I, personally, like a lady who plans ahead."

"What makes you think I give a hoot what you like, Mr. Turner?"

"You mean you don't?"

"No!"

"Does that mean you're not going to tell me who the lucky guy is?"

"There is no 'guy.' I do not go out with 'guys.'"

"Then who *do* you go out with?"

"That's none of your business."

"But there is somebody, right?"

Underneath the needling was genuine curiosity. While Jake had done a bit of nosing around since his arrival, he'd been unable to discover whether Callie had a man in her life. All indications were that she didn't, but Jake wasn't ready to buy that. For all her prickly ways, Callie Barnwell didn't strike him as a dried-up spinster. She was a vibrant, flesh-and-blood female. He found it impossible to believe that the local good old boys had overlooked her.

"I said—"

"C'mon, Callie," Jake urged, grinning wickedly. "You tell me about yours, I'll tell you about mine."

"I have absolutely no desire to listen to a single syllable about your sordid affairs," she spat at him.

Once again Jake noticed how anger intensified Callie's drawl. He wondered fleetingly whether other strong emotions—passion, for instance—had the same effect.

"Well, you must have listened to something if you know enough to call them sordid," he observed provocatively.

"You are dis—" her voice caught. She swallowed convulsively. "Disgustin'!"

There was a suspicious sheen in Callie's eyes. While her cheeks were bright pink, the rest of her face had gone milky pale. Jake could see the rapid rise and fall of her breasts beneath the pristine white fabric of her short-sleeved blouse. With a pang of shame, he realized he'd shoved her right to the brink of tears.

"Hey, Callie—" he began guiltily, reaching out to her. He wanted to apologize.

She recoiled. "Get away from me."

Jake withdrew his extended hand and hooked his thumbs through two of the belt loops on the waistband of his jeans. He rocked back on his heels. All right. He'd soothe her first, then he'd say he was sorry.

"Don't you think you're overreacting a little?" he asked after a brief pause.

Callie sliced him from head to toe with a razor-sharp look. "You think I'm overreacting because I don't want a man who believes I'm ready to have sex at the drop of a pair of pants anywhere near me?" she demanded.

Jake shook his head in vehement denial. "I *never* implied anything like that."

"You most certainly did, Mr. Turner."

He clenched his fingers, his good intentions of just a few seconds before going out the window. "Jake, dammit! My name is *Jake*. J-A-K-E."

"No," she flung back at him. "Your name is *mud!* M-U-D!"

They glared at each other. It was clear to Jake that Callie was no longer in danger of breaking into tears. She was simply gloriously, gorgeously, enraged.

The hackneyed line "Gee, you're beautiful when you're angry" flitted through Jake's mind, but he swatted it away like a mosquito. He figured Callie would haul off and smack him if he said something like that at this point. He also figured he wouldn't blame her one bit if she did.

Jake saw her hazel eyes narrow suddenly and wondered if his expression had betrayed the direction of his thoughts. Her chin went up a notch and she shifted her weight, obviously bracing herself.

Neither of them spoke for at least thirty seconds.

"When I mentioned your overreacting," Jake said finally, "I was referring to P.D.'s condom."

Callie stiffened. One of her hands moved to cover the skirt pocket she'd shoved the small packet into. She remained silent.

"That *is* what you were upset about when I walked in, wasn't it?" Jake pursued. "Finding a condom in P.D.'s jeans?"

"How—?"

Jake's mouth twisted. "I didn't really think it was yours, Callie. And I knew it wasn't mine because frankly—or crudely, if you prefer—I don't use that brand."

Callie swallowed. "I...see."

"Look, just because P.D.'s carrying condoms doesn't mean he's using them."

"I never thought—"

"Yes, you did. And it shocked the hell out of you. Because you still consider P.D. a kid. But he's not. He's sixteen."

"I'm aware of how old my brother is, thank you very much. I've been raising him since he was ten!"

"I'm not criticizing the way you've raised him," Jake declared quickly. He was telling the truth. It was obvious that P. D. Barnwell had been brought up to have the right stuff. But it was also obvious that the teenager was restless and ripe for rebellion. If his half sister kept treating him like a child, P.D. would undoubtedly end up doing his damnedest to prove how grown-up he was.

"I can't tell you how relieved I am to hear that," Callie retorted. "I'd hate to think that an expert like yourself—"

"Look, I never claimed to be an expert," Jake interrupted in an exasperated tone. "I'd be the first one to admit I know diddly about raising kids. But the fact is, I *do*

know a whole bunch about being a sixteen-year-old boy. I've
been one and, believe me, the experience sticks with you.
Now, it's possible P.D.'s carrying condoms because he's
having sex and he wants to make sure he and his girl are
protected. If that's the case—well, he's acting more respon-
sibly than a lot of so-called adults. It's also possible—
probable, if you want my opinion—that the only reason he's
got rubbers is that he wants to convince his buddies he's a
stud.''

Jake kept his eyes fixed on Callie's face as he spoke. He
could tell she didn't relish hearing what he was telling her.
He could also tell she recognized the validity of his words.

She remained silent for several long moments after he
finished speaking. The defensiveness had drained out of her.
She suddenly looked very vulnerable.

Jake found himself thinking about the kinds of burdens
Callie had been shouldering for the past six years. He also
found himself wondering if he might be able to do anything
to lighten her load while he was around. The possibility was
appealing... and appalling. It implied making the kind of
emotional connection he'd always steered clear of.

Callie sighed and averted her face. Her gaze slid away
from Jake's.

"He... he doesn't really talk to me anymore," she confessed with an awkward gesture. "P.D., I mean. Oh, we still
have conversations. But we don't seem to... to communi-
cate like we used to."

Jake hesitated for a few seconds, then slowly raised his
right hand. He placed his fingertips against one side of
Callie's jaw and gently urged her face toward his. He
thought he felt her tremble in the first instant he touched
her. He saw her lips part slightly as their eyes met.

The lambent morning sunlight streaming in from the
kitchen windows did lovely things to Callie's skin and hair.
Jake could have spent a long time considering them, but he
knew that wouldn't be wise. He cleared his throat.

"Look," he said quietly, "would you like me to have a
little man-to-man—"

Jake stopped speaking as he heard the kitchen door open.

"Why, good mornin', Jacob. Good mornin', Callie," Henrietta Penelope Barnwell chirped cheerfully. "I *thought* I heard the two of you in here!"

Lord, give me patience, Callie prayed silently about five hours later. And give it to me right this instant!

She was in the middle of a consultation with none other than the cleavage-conscious Miss Janie Mae Winslow. They'd adjourned to her tiny office in the rear of Callie's Corner roughly twenty minutes before to examine some sketches and swatches.

"Hmm...hmmm...hmmmm," Janie Mae hummed, tapping one perfectly manicured nail against a flawlessly capped front tooth.

Callie heard the silvery jingle that announced the arrival of a new customer. She'd left the door of her office open so she could keep an eye on her shop and her sales clerk, Sage Bolling. Looking up from the drawings spread across her desk, she saw a woman enter the store and make a beeline for the sale rack. She returned her attention to the work at hand.

"Callie, sugar," Janie Mae drawled languidly, "I just love this blue." She indicated a square of sapphire-hued satin.

"That's twenty-six ninety-five a yard, Janie Mae," Callie informed her.

Janie Mae dismissed the price with an airy wave, then cocked her raven-haired head to one side. "I had my colors done, you know. I'm a Classic Winter. And that's the exact shade of blue I'm s'posed to wear."

"Wonderful," Callie responded. "Now, what about the designs?"

"Well, I'm not sure what to think. I mean, I like the sleeves on this first one. With those cute double puffs, they look kind of like peanut shells, you know? And I adore the drapin' on the skirt of the third one. I simply can't abide a gown that hangs straight down like a flour sack. Still—and

I don't want you to think I'm findin' fault—none of these designs truly cries out to me."

Callie suppressed a sigh. "Let me guess. You have a problem with the necklines, right?"

Janie Mae smiled. "Don't you think they ought to be a teeny-tiny bit lower?" she asked winsomely. "Now, I realize you're the expert when it comes to dress designin', Callie. After all, you did study at that fashion institution up in New York City. But *I* happen to be somethin' of an authority on beauty pageants. And I know for a fact that a girl isn't going to get crowned if she covers up her best attributes."

Callie kept her eyes resolutely fixed on the sketches. "Janie Mae, if you put on a gown with a neckline any lower than the ones I've drawn, your best attributes are going to fall out."

The erstwhile Peanut Princess laughed. "No, they won't."

Startled, Callie looked up into Janie Mae's heart-shaped face. "Yes, they will. There are certain physical laws—"

"I'm going to use stick-em."

Callie blinked. She dimly registered the tinkling of the bell hung over the front door. "You—what?"

"I'm going to use stick-em," the brunette repeated smugly. "Don't you remember? I told you about that stuff I spray on my rear end to keep my swimsuit from ridin' up when I'm on the runway?"

"Ah...vaguely."

"Well, I figure that what works on my behind will work on my baz—" Janie Mae broke off, her gaze homing in on something out in the shop. "Lordy, Lordy," she breathed reverently. "Now that's what I call a *man.*"

Callie felt a shocking surge of physical awareness.

Oh, no.

She turned.

Oh, yes.

"That's him, isn't it," Janie Mae whispered excitedly. "That's the Yankee you've got livin' with you! I heard all

about him yesterday at the beauty parlor. He *does* look a
little like that pencil sketch of Harriman—"

"Excuse me, Janie Mae," Callie interrupted. "I'll be
back in just a minute."

What in the world was Jake Turner doing in her shop? she
wondered, walking out of her office on legs that seemed
curiously unstable. Her first thought was that there must be
something wrong with her aunt or P.D., but nothing about
Jake's manner communicated urgency. Indeed, he was loi-
tering near the front of the shop, looking as out of place as
a tomcat in a hen house.

He was drawing glances from Callie's customers the way
a magnet draws iron. Most of the women in the shop were
trying to disguise their interest. Not so her sales clerk. Sage
was gawking at Jake, eyes huge, mouth hanging open.

"You're drooling down the front of your new blouse,
Sage," Callie murmured as she moved by the young woman.

It seemed to take her a ridiculously long time to reach
Jake. She was relieved to note that he'd at least had the de-
cency to put on a shirt some time in the last five hours. One
of the many things that had unnerved her about their encounter in the kitchen had been the fact that he'd been clad
in nothing but shoes and jeans.

Of course, the top he was wearing now wasn't the most
modest garment he could have chosen. It did very little to
hide the muscled virility of his torso and shoulders. It was
also unbuttoned to his breastbone, revealing a hair-
roughened triangle of sun-bronzed skin.

Callie saw Jake square his broad shoulders and take a
deep breath as she came to within touching distance. There
was an odd expression flickering in the depths of his blue-
green eyes. The arrogant assurance she'd come to associate
with him had been replaced by an aura of uncertainty. He
seemed . . . nervous.

"May I help you, Mr. Turner?" she asked after a moment.

Jake's well-shaped lips twisted briefly at her use of his surname. "I certainly hope so, Miss Barnwell," he returned.

Callie lifted her brows, inviting him to be specific.

"You can help me by accepting my apology for what happened this morning in the kitchen."

Callie blinked, unable to believe she'd heard him correctly. If she'd made up a list of all the things she expected to come out of Jake Turner's mouth, an apology wouldn't have been on it.

"I . . . I don't . . ."

"I was way out of line," he said flatly, cutting across her fragmented attempt to respond. If he was aware of the attention he was attracting, he gave no sign of it. "I'm sorry."

Callie was torn by a variety of conflicting emotions. It was very difficult for her to trust Jake Turner. The man had given her nothing but grief since he'd barged into her house and life. And yet, she couldn't deny that he looked and sounded sincerely regretful. She also had to concede that his manner toward her was the essence of gentlemanly respect.

Callie's mind replayed pieces of their encounter in the kitchen. Lord knew, the man had plenty to apologize for! Although, to be fair, he'd started seeming almost . . . well, almost *tolerable* just before her aunt had walked in. He'd appeared to be genuinely concerned about P.D. In fact, there'd been a few moments when she'd actually gotten the impression that he'd been concerned about her, too!

She opened her mouth to speak then hesitated, recalling Sunday School lessons about the need for Christian forgiveness. She also recalled the Biblical admonition about he without sin being the one to cast the first stone. Her innate honesty forced her to acknowledge that she'd been at fault this morning, too.

"Well," she began, making a little gesture, "I wasn't exactly—"

"Oh, no." Jake shook his head. One corner of his mouth quirked up, creating a crease in his tanned cheek. "I've spent the last five hours wallowing in the idea that what happened was all my fault. Please, don't try to relieve me of my guilt.'' The quirk became more marked, the crease deepened. ''I don't usually admit to being in the wrong, you know.''

A sudden laugh tickled the back of Callie's throat. The man was outrageous, she thought. Absolutely outrageous! Most folks would have been more than willing to white-wash their mistakes. But not Jake Turner! No, he wanted to paint himself as even blacker then he really was.

''I find it hard to imagine that you've *ever* admitted it, Mr. Turner,'' she answered. There was a bantering note in her voice.

Jake chuckled briefly, then grew serious once more. ''Look, I *am* sorry,'' he told her, scrutinizing her face. ''I hope you believe me.''

Callie looked down for a moment, unable—or, perhaps, unwilling—to sustain the sudden intensity of his gaze. She searched around for the resentment and hostility she'd felt toward Jake earlier. She couldn't find them. She wasn't prepared to name the feelings she discovered instead.

''Callie?'' he questioned.

She lifted her gaze back to his. She knew her customers were watching because she could feel the weight of their curious stares. She didn't want to think about how quickly word of Jake's appearance in Callie's Corner was going to spread. It would probably be all over town before nightfall. And heaven only knew how twisted and exaggerated the account would be by that time!

''I believe you,'' she returned simply. ''I accept your apology.''

Jake expelled his breath as though he'd been holding it while waiting for her response. ''Thank you,'' he said and flashed her a smile.

Callie felt the impact of that smile right down to her toes. She reciprocated with one of her own. She couldn't help herself. ''You're welcome,'' she said a bit breathily.

There was a short pause.

"Will you have lunch with me?" Jake asked abruptly, thrusting his hands into his pockets as though he wasn't quite sure what to do with them.

"Lunch?" Callie echoed. The word came out a lot more loudly than she'd intended it to. She winced inwardly, trying not to imagine the kind of speculative frenzy this single syllable would spark in the women who'd just heard it.

"You haven't eaten, have you? I know it's nearly one—"

"No, I haven't eaten," she told him, dropping her voice to near-whisper level. "But—"

"Would you have lunch with me, then?" he interrupted. "Between beating myself up about the way I acted and installing about a mile of molding, I've worked up quite an appetite. I thought we could go to the place down the street—Earle's All You Can Eat."

Callie experienced a real pang of disappointment. She knew the feeling wasn't due solely to the prospect of having to miss out on Earle Barnett's excellent cooking.

"I can't," she said.

Jake stiffened, his spine and shoulders going rigid. "Can't or won't?" he asked pointedly.

She hesitated, understanding what a difference her answer might make.

"I can't," she finally repeated, meeting his eyes very steadily. "I have customers to take care of. I'm sorry."

Callie saw the tension seep out of the lines of Jake's body. He stayed silent for several seconds, as though he was debating what he was going to say next. Finally, he took his hands out of his pockets and spoke.

"Would you have lunch with me if you *didn't* have customers to take care of?" he questioned softly.

Again she hesitated. Her pulse accelerated. She felt warm and a little weak.

"Callie?" he prompted, his voice even softer than it had been a moment before.

Callie made up her mind.

"Yes, Jake," she replied, giving him a slow smile. "I believe I would."

Four

———

Jake had discovered Earle's All You Can Eat Café during his previous stay in the Deacon's Crossing area. He'd had lunch there twice in the past week. But while the food had been as delicious as he'd remembered it, the atmosphere had definitely changed.

When he'd patronized the place two months before, he'd simply drawn a few questioning glances and a couple of brief nods of greeting. No one had seemed particularly affected—or offended—by his presence.

The reception he'd received when he'd gone back to the café two days after moving into the Barnwell house had been radically different. Every conversation in the place had stopped dead when he'd walked in. He'd found himself the target of intense scrutiny from at least a dozen pairs of eyes.

The same thing had happened the next time he'd gone to Earle's. And damned if it didn't happen again when he walked in a few minutes after his encounter with Callie!

If he hadn't felt so pleased by what had taken place in Callie's Corner, Jake probably would have been irritated by the reception. Although he wasn't particularly concerned about local opinion of him—he was, after all, going to be gone by September—he didn't much enjoy being treated like a freak. Still, his mood on this sunshiny July afternoon was such that he found it easy to shrug off the stares and the unnatural silence.

Moving to the far end of the café's Formica-covered counter, Jake lowered himself onto the last stool. A rotund older man in a three-piece white linen suit was perched on the stool to his left. A small blackboard listing the daily specials was hanging on the wall to his right. Jake glanced over the offerings absently, mentally replaying the scene in Callie's dress shop.

It would be a long time before he forgot the slow, sweet smile Callie had given him when she'd admitted that she would've accepted his invitation if she'd been able to. The admission alone would have made his day, but to also have the memory of that smile. . . .

She hadn't just smiled with her lips, either. No, there'd been a smile in the depths of her lovely, gray-green eyes, too.

Jake couldn't help wondering what that smile might have led to had he and Callie had a little more time and a lot more privacy. He certainly had no doubts about where he would have *liked* to have—

Jake broke off this line of thought as he realized that the portly patron sitting to his left was addressing him. He swiveled his stool so he could look at the man.

"I do hope you'll excuse me interruptin' your contemplations," the gentleman said in a mellifluous voice. "But I was wonderin' if I might trouble you to pass me the pepper sauce for my greens?" He inclined his balding head first toward a row of bottles sitting on the end of the counter, then toward the side dish of turnip greens he'd been served along with a plate of baked ham and yams.

"No trouble," Jake replied, handing over one of the small glass containers. He watched as the man drenched his greens with the condiment. Jake's mouth started to tingle.

He'd tried a dash of the pepper sauce on something two months before. The searing taste had blistered his tongue.

The man sampled his greens with the intensity of a wine connoisseur sipping a rare vintage, eyes closed, expression intent.

"Heavenly," he declared after he'd chewed and swallowed. "I must remember to extend my compliments to the chef." He smiled at Jake. "By the way, my name is Bates. Augustus Bates. I own and operate our local paper."

"Mr. Bates," Jake acknowledged with a nod, carefully schooling his features into neutrality. He'd gotten an earful about the publisher of the *Deacon's Crossing Weekly* from Miss Henny during the past seven days. But what he'd heard didn't jibe with the man he saw sitting next to him. Augustus Bates certainly didn't look like the embodiment of First Amendment evil. "I'm Jake Turner."

"Oh, yes," came the placid response, "I know."

"How the—"

"Everythin' all right with you, Mr. Bates?" the waitress who was working the counter interrupted. A buxom woman in her late forties, she favored pale blue eyeshadow and iridescent pink nail polish. Her beehive coiffure demonstrated that, given enough hairspray, it was possible to defy the law of gravity. Jake vaguely recalled that he'd been served by her the first time he'd patronized Earle's.

"I am enraptured by today's culinary offerin's, Bernice," the older man returned.

Bernice arched her carefully penciled brows. "Is that good or bad?"

"Good."

Bernice transferred her attention to Jake. "And how can we enrapture *you* today, sugar?"

Jake glanced back at the blackboard menu for a moment. "I'll have a bowl of Brunswick stew and some cornbread, please."

"The stew's made with chicken, not squirrel," Bernice warned. She sounded as though she expected him to change his mind once he heard this.

"That's fine."

"Unsweetened tea to drink, right?"

"Right." Jake was taken aback that she'd remembered his preference. He knew the tea would come iced. It always did south of the Mason-Dixon line unless *hot* tea was specified.

Bernice seemed to divine his feelings. "I never forget an order, hon," she declared with a smile, then sashayed off.

Augustus Bates ate a morsel of ham, then dabbed at his mouth with a napkin. He wielded the paper square as though it were the finest Irish linen. "I believe you were on the verge of inquirin' how I happen to be familiar with your identity, Mr. Turner," he commented.

"Something like that," Jake conceded.

"It troubles you that I am?"

Jake glanced around, unsure how to answer this blunt question. He noted that the café's customers had started talking to each other again. He would have been pleased had he not had the unsettling feeling that he was the main topic of most of their discussions.

The newspaperman continued speaking. "If you came to Deacon's Crossin' seekin' anonymity, Mr. Turner, I fear you're destined for disappointment. You've become—obviously without intendin'—somethin' of a celebrity."

Jake stared. "A *celebrity?*" He gave a distracted nod to Bernice, who'd just bustled back to the counter with his beverage.

"Why, yes," Bates affirmed. "Your residence with the Barnwells has earned you a certain degree of fame hereabouts. You see, it's been more than a century since the ladies of that esteemed family opened their doors to a man who wasn't related to them by blood."

"Now, Mr. Bates, that's just not so," Bernice objected before Jake had a chance to react. "Callie and Miss Henny rented a room to that oral history fella from Massachusetts last year. You remember, the one John Thomas accidentally stuck with a sword durin' rehearsal for the Founders' Day Festival?"

"I remember Dr. Goldfluss vividly, my dear Bernice. But I don't believe his stay with the Barnwells invalidates my assertion." The older man looked at Jake. "Dr. Goldfluss was much more capon than cock of the walk, if you discern my drift."

It took Jake a moment, but he decided he did.

"You sound as though you know a great deal about the Barnwell ladies, Mr. Bates," he said slowly, wary of appearing too inquisitive. He sensed that something about him had gained Mr. Bates's approval, but he didn't want to press his luck.

The older man's mouth curved into a knowing smile. "You sound as though you don't, but would like to, Mr. Turner."

"Well, I can tell you one thing right off," Bernice declared, planting her palms on the counter. "The Barnwell women are unlucky in love. Why, take Miss Henny—"

"I truly do not think that will be necessary, Bernice," the publisher of the *Deacon's Crossing Weekly* said.

Jake's gaze darted between the waitress and newspaperman. He got the distinct impression that Augustus Bates was trying to protect Henrietta Barnwell's reputation. But why would the man want to do that?

"All right, all right," Bernice said, flushing slightly. "Take Callie, then."

"*What?*" Jake went rigid, abandoning his speculation about Mr. Bates and Miss Henny.

Bernice shot him a sharp look. "Poor thing was deserted by her fancy fiancé in her time of tribulation," she informed him dramatically. "I swear to you, the Barnwell women have been doomed to die spinsters ever since Caroline Anne Barnwell was done dirt by that Yankee bastard, Harriman Gage."

"So that's Harriman Gage, hmm?" Jake said a week later, scrutinizing the silver-framed pencil sketch he'd just removed from the top shelf of a large breakfront cabinet located in the Barnwells' parlor.

"That picture dates from the Christmas of eighteen hundred and seventy-four," Callie's aunt noted, hovering anxiously at his elbow. She was supervising the emptying of the cabinet.

Jake nodded, continued to examine the faded drawing. The face depicted in it was bearded, angular and, he supposed, attractive. He detected very little similarity between the old-fashioned visage and the reflection he saw in the bathroom mirror each morning.

"Do you really think I look like him, Miss Henny?" he inquired, glancing at the older woman.

Henny made a fluttery gesture. "Now, Jacob," she chided. "It isn't gentlemanly of you to remind me of my foolishness. I swear, I could perish from humiliation every time I think of how I behaved the night you arrived here. It's not as though I put any stock in that old tale about Harriman Gage's restless spirit roamin' around seekin' eternal rest! Still, there's no denyin' I suffered a shock when I answered the door two weeks ago. I was distracted. The lightin' was bad what with the storm and all. And there you loomed up before me, big as life and as wet as could be..." She let her voice trail off.

Jake flashed Henny a quick smile and handed over the drawing. "Don't let it bother you," he said easily. He wondered fleetingly what his having been wet had to do with her mistaking him for some guy who'd come back from the grave, but decided he could live without knowing.

"I don't see much of a resemblance now that you've shaved and had your hair trimmed a little," the older woman conceded, looking from the sketch to Jake. She frowned consideringly. "Although...there's *still* somethin' about your mouth that reminds me of his."

Jake let a few moments pass, running his fingers assessingly over the hinges of the breakfront's cabinet doors. Two of them definitely needed replacing. He added this to his lengthening mental list of things to do around the house.

"You know, Miss Henny," he commented reflectively, "I'm a little surprised your family's kept that sketch all these years."

"Why, it's an heirloom," the older woman responded, her tone suggesting that should explain everything. "Like Caroline Anne's diaries." She gestured toward the set of leather-bound journals Jake had removed from the cabinet a short time before and stacked on the parlor love seat.

"But considering what Harriman Gage did . . ."

Jake was angling for facts. He had yet to discover precisely how Harriman Gage had wronged Caroline Anne Barnwell. While Augustus Bates and Bernice the waitress had been remarkably forthcoming about a lot of things during their conversation at Earle's the week before, they'd danced around that particular subject. Jake had found himself surprisingly reluctant to press the matter with them.

He was even more inhibited when it came to raising the issue around the Barnwells. Although he'd come close to asking P.D. a couple of times, he'd always backed off at the last instant. He realized that his reticence was a little strange, given the frankness of the discussions he and the teenager had had during the past seven days.

"Not everythin' that happens to a family is pleasant, Jacob," Henny told him, offering philosophy rather than information. "We have to acknowledge the bad to appreciate the good. And speakin' of families, I'd truly love to hear a little about yours. You've been awfully close-mouthed about your people, you know."

The shift of conversational direction caught Jake flat-footed. He usually sensed personal inquiries coming a mile away and deflected them before they were asked. It shook him to realize how much he'd let his guard down during the past fourteen days.

"I don't have a family," he answered tersely. His tone was blunt, almost brutal. It was a far cry from the one he'd gotten into the habit of using around Callie's aunt.

"You mean, you're an orphan?"

"More or less."

Henny looked puzzled. "I don't understand."

Jake thrust the fingers of one hand back through his hair. He had a sharp, sudden urge to tell the older woman that his family—or lack of it—was none of her damned business. He fought down the impulse, knowing he would hurt Henny by saying something like that.

But he also knew he would hurt her by telling her the entire truth. While he'd come to the conclusion that Henrietta Penelope Barnwell was far less of a featherbrain than she seemed, he'd also realized she was a gentle soul who had no sense of how truly cruel the world could be. How could she understand the ugliness of a fourteen-year marriage between a wealthy alcoholic husband and a flagrantly unfaithful wife? How could she understand the damage that had been done to the only child of that loveless union?

"My father's dead," he said finally. "And my mother is...someplace...with her third or fourth husband."

There was a brief silence.

"You don't want to talk about it," Henny said eventually.

"I don't think you want to hear about it."

"I see." She cocked her head. "You don't have any brothers or sisters? Aunts or uncles? Cousins?"

"No."

"Why, you poor thing."

Jake stiffened. He liked Henrietta Barnwell. Against all odds, he genuinely liked her. But he wasn't going to accept her pity. He also had no intention of letting her go running to her niece with some sob story about his empty and unhappy personal life.

"I do all right, Miss Henny," he said flatly.

"Goodness, I never thought you didn't!" Henny replied with a trace of asperity. Callie's aunt was normally as pleasant as she was plump, but Jake had discovered she could turn prickly when she felt she was being misunderstood. "From the instant I saw you—well, no, not from the *exact* instant—but just as soon as I made your acquaintance, I knew you were a man of good, strong character.

Character's what counts in the world, if you ask my opinion. And you've got talent, too. P.D. told me somethin' you built is on display at a museum in Washington, D.C.''

Jake blinked. He'd forgotten the kid knew about that. He kept a three-ring binder containing photographs and slides of his work, and P.D. had seen it while helping him unload the back of the pickup the night he'd arrived. The teenager had asked a lot of questions about what he did for a living.

The "something" to which Miss Henny had just referred was a lavishly carved console table he'd made for a collector in Boston about nine years before. The table—which had helped establish his reputation and led to a string of lucrative commissions—was currently on loan to a traveling exhibit showcasing American craftsmen.

"Callie had two of her dresses on display in the front window of one of those fancy stores on Fifth Avenue once," Henny went on. "She'd won this designin' contest and that was part of the prize."

Jake was more than happy to get off the subject of him and onto the subject of Miss Henny's niece.

"This was when she was studying fashion in New York?" he asked, keeping his voice casual. He made a show of examining a series of blisters that marred the veneered surface of the breakfront. While P.D. had provided him with some details about Callie's professional training, he wanted to know more.

"That's right," Henny confirmed. "It was before the tragedy with my brother and his second wife." She heaved a sad sigh. "You know, Jacob, there's just no tellin' how far that dear child would have gone if she hadn't had to come back to Deacon's Crossing and take on the burden of lookin' after all of us."

"What the—" Callie muttered when she turned into the driveway of her house a few minutes later.

She'd had a long, hard Saturday at Callie's Corner. A Saturday crammed full of inconvenience, irritation and aggravation. Right now her feet hurt. Her temples throbbed.

She was in no mood to find that she couldn't pull into the garage because the entrance was being blocked by her half brother and Jake Turner's big, black motorcycle.

P.D. wasn't on the Harley-Davidson. No, he was on his knees next to the damned thing! He appeared to be washing it. Then again, given his attitude toward the machine, he might very well be worshiping it.

Callie got out of her car and marched forward. "P.D., what are you doing?" she demanded, coming to a halt about a foot from the front of the motorcycle.

The teenager looked up. "Hey, Callie," he greeted her casually. "What I'm doin' is cleanin' Jake's hog."

"Did he tell you to do that?" While Callie knew her feelings toward Jake had warmed up during the past week, she was still very wary of the influence the man seemed to exert over her half brother.

"'Course not," the teenager answered. "I asked him if I could. He let me take another little ride this afternoon, see. And yeah, before you ask, I wore a helmet. Jake says only hard heads don't wear helmets and hard heads get soft real fast when they hit the highway. Anyway, when I got back from ridin', I noticed the Harley was kind of dusty. So, here I am." He gestured with a hand that held a small, soapy sponge.

"Don't you have anything better to do?"

"Like what?"

Callie searched for a response, nettled that nothing came immediately to mind.

"Yeah, that's what I thought," P.D. sniped.

Stung, Callie leaned over and flipped a lock of hair back from her half brother's forehead. "Well, you could always get a haircut."

P.D. glared at her. "There's nothin' wrong with my hair."

"It's hanging over your ears and collar!"

"I like it hangin'! I want it to look just like Jake's."

Oh, yes, of course, Callie thought, struggling to control her temper. He wanted it to look just like Jake's. She should have known. He'd already taken to wearing white T-shirts and low-riding jeans *just like Jake's*. He'd adopted a thumbs-through-the-belt-loops stance that was *just like Jake's,* too. He'd even tried to change his way of walking. Whether he'd ever develop a powerful, coiled spring stride that was *just like Jake's* remained to be seen.

"P.D.—" she began.

"I'm old enough to decide how I'm goin' to have my hair," he interrupted. "I'm not a kid!"

"I don't think you're—"

"Oh, yes, you do so!" he accused. His throat worked, his mouth twisted. Then, he declared tightly, "Aunt Henny's goin' to have supper ready soon and I want to get this finished up before she calls. Just leave me alone, Callie."

Not knowing what else to do, Callie did.

Jake recognized that Callie was upset the instant he saw her, but his efforts to find out what was wrong were instantly and absolutely rebuffed. Despite her refusal to answer his questions, he made a few educated guesses about what was going on. These guesses were confirmed when P.D. came slamming into the house about five minutes after his half sister went stomping up to her second-floor bedroom.

They all had supper in the kitchen. The atmosphere at the table was extremely uncomfortable, although Miss Henny did everything in her power to keep the conversational ball rolling. Jake's admiration for the older woman increased tremendously during the meal. And, while he'd never had much use for chitchat, he found himself actively supporting her attempt to maintain some semblance of normality.

A particularly strained silence descended as they were finishing dessert. Responding to a pleading look from Miss Henny, Jake cast around for something to say that might lessen the tension. He ended up inviting Callie to take a drive with him after the supper dishes were done. He told himself that getting her out of the house and away from P.D. would relax her. He did not examine what having an op-

portunity to spend some time alone with the lady might do
for him.

Callie's rejection of his idea was unequivocal. The split
second she finished voicing it, P.D. excused himself and
bolted upstairs.

Jake Turner had spent his childhood and much of his adolescence living in places that were much more battle-
grounds for emotional warfare than homes. While he'd
mastered the tactics of confrontation, he'd also learned the
benefits of strategic withdrawal. So once he'd helped clear
the table and assured himself that Miss Henny was capable
of weathering the storm between her niece and nephew on
her own, he took off on his motorcycle.

He headed the Harley for a small roadhouse he'd found
during his previous stint in the area. It was just about eight
when he pulled up in front of the place. While it was obvious from the traffic in the parking lot that business was
brisk, Jake knew things would get a whole lot livelier before Saturday night gave way to Sunday morning.

Once inside he ran into a couple of other subcontractors
who were working on the Belle Terre project. He spent the
next few hours with them nursing a pair of beers and listening to some nitty-gritty country music.

Jake walked out of the roadhouse feeling a lot looser than
he'd felt when he'd walked in. The only thing he had to
complain about was that some boozed-up lummox had accidentally dumped a shot of bourbon on him.

Jake was vaguely aware that the smell of the spilled liquor was still pretty strong when he arrived back at the
Barnwell house about half-past midnight. He decided he
needed to take a shower before he turned in. The shirt he
was wearing could use a wash, too. There was no point in
tossing it into the laundry the way it was. If he did that,
Callie would get hold of it, take one sniff and once again
decide his name was M-U-D.

This was assuming, of course, that she hadn't reverted to
that way of thinking already. Given her behavior before and
during supper, it seemed entirely possible she had.

Jake turned his motorcycle into the gravel-covered driveway, his gaze flicking upward to check the second-story window that had given him his first, unforgettable glimpse of Callie Barnwell. The window was dark, indicating she was probably in bed and asleep.

Jake became aware of a sudden tightening in his groin.

What, he wondered, did Callie wear at night? Something sheer and sexy? Something ladylike with a demure touch of lace? Or maybe she snuggled into an oversized T-shirt like the one she'd had on—

And then Jake saw it. A body. It was spread-eagled on the driveway about fifteen feet in front of him.

P.D.

Oh, God. It was P.D.!

Jake brought the Harley to a skidding stop, sending small stones spraying out in all directions like shrapnel. He killed the engine and booted the kickstand into place. A split second later he was off the bike.

For one gut-wrenching moment, Jake was afraid the kid was dead. Then he got close enough to see the rise and fall of the teenager's chest. An instant later, he was close enough to smell the unmistakable odor of cheap booze.

Swearing under his breath, Jake dropped to his knees beside P.D.'s prone body. He undid the chin strap of the helmet he was wearing and pulled it off. The kid's dead all right, he thought. Dead *drunk*.

"P.D.," he said sharply. The night was clear and the moon overhead was full. There was more than enough light to determine that the teenager bore no visible cuts or bruises.

P.D. stirred and grunted something incomprehensible. His eyes were closed, his features slack.

"P.D.," Jake repeated, prodding the kid's shoulder. "Hey. Palmer Dean."

Callie's half brother stirred again. After a moment, he opened his eyes. "Whozzat?" he asked. "Jake? Izzatchoo Jake?"

"Yeah, kid," Jake confirmed. "It's me."

P.D.'s eyes wavered for a second, then focused. A smile oozed from one corner of his mouth to the other. "Jake! My goo' buddy Jake!"

Jake grimaced. "P.D., what the hell do you think you're doing?"

"Doin'? Whadduzzit loo' li-ike? I'm havin' a goo' time."

"Does Callie know you went out tonight?" Even as he asked it, Jake realized it was a pretty stupid question.

P.D. let his head flop back and forth several times. "I crawl oudda win'ow," he answered smugly. "Go see my bes' frien', Seth. Seth Avery. Wen' out tonigh' with him 'n' somma m'other buddies." He grinned stupidly for a second or two, then his expression turned mulish. "Thinks I'm stilla kid," he muttered darkly. "I'm *nodda* kid. Gonna show *her.*"

Jake sighed and raked his hair with his fingers. "Yeah, P.D.," he responded trenchantly. "Getting smashed is just the ticket to showing Callie how mature you are."

"Huh?"

"Never mind. Never mind."

Jake considered the situation for a moment. It didn't require a Ph.D. in psychology to figure out what had happened. He'd warned Callie she had to stop treating her half brother like a little boy, but she hadn't gotten the message. She simply hadn't realized the kind of trouble an adolescent male could get into trying to prove he was a man.

Letting Callie see P.D. in his current condition would be the most effective "I told you so" Jake could imagine. But he couldn't do it. He couldn't hurt or humiliate her that way. He couldn't do it because—dammit!—he wanted to help her.

Oh, hell, he wanted to do a lot more than help her and he knew it!

"Jake?" P.D. inquired.

"Right here, kid," Jake replied, making up his mind.

"D'you thin' I'm really drunk, Jake?"

"Yeah, kid. I think you're really drunk."

"Never been really drunk b'fore."

"Glad to hear it. You get really drunk again and I'm going to kick your sixteen-year-old butt. This time, though, I'm going to save it."

"Wha—?"

"I'm going to lug you into the house, clean you up and dump you in bed. And tomorrow when you're hung over I'm going to help you convince Callie you've got some kind of virus."

"I'm gonna be hun' over?"

Jake smiled briefly. "Kid, you're going to be so sick you'll have to make a recovery to feel good enough to die."

Jake got P.D. off the ground and slung over his shoulder all right, although his balance was a bit dicey. He made it onto the porch just fine, then experienced a problem trying to fish his key to the front door out of his back jeans pocket.

"Can I do some'in' to he'p?" P.D. inquired loudly, suddenly coming to life.

Jake started, nearly losing his footing. He'd thought the kid had passed out!

"Yeah, you can do something to help," he whispered fiercely, locating the key and pulling it out. It took him a long and fumbling moment to fit it into the lock. "You can stop squirming and shut up."

"But—"

"Not a word, P.D.! I don't want you to say one word from now on!"

The front door swung open. Jake silently congratulated himself for having taken the time to oil its hinges several days before.

"Don' worry, Jake," P.D. muttered from his upside-down position. "Not gonna say 'nother word. Gonna sing a l'il ole Elvis song instead."

Five

"What was I supposed to think?" Callie asked unhappily, plopping a lump of lard into a bowl containing flour, baking soda, baking powder and salt. Reaching to her right, she yanked open a drawer and extracted a fork. After slamming the drawer shut, she began using the utensil to cut the shortening into the dry ingredients.

"Really," she went on rhetorically, wielding the fork with far more force than was necessary. "What was I supposed to think? First I'm woken up by the sound of that damned motorcycle. Then I hear P.D. caterwauling "Heartbreak Hotel." So, naturally, I get up to see what's going on. And what do I find? Why, I find Jake Turner in the front hallway with my sixteen-year-old brother draped over his shoulder! And not only is the man having trouble standing up, but he stinks to high heaven of liquor!"

Callie closed her eyes for a moment, summoning up the scene.

"*What do you think you're doing?*" She'd gasped, utterly appalled by what she was seeing.

Jake's eyes had connected with hers for an electrified instant. He'd obviously been shocked and dismayed to see her.

"—*duh-duh duh-duh duh . . .*" P.D. had crooned, flinging his arms out to the sides. Jake had staggered slightly.

"*Well?*" she'd whispered furiously, praying her aunt would remain asleep and unaware on the second floor. That Jake Turner had decided to go out, get drunk and then come stumbling into their home was awful enough. That he'd lured P.D. into joining him was unforgivable! Callie had known such a betrayal of trust would devastate her Aunt Henny.

"*What do you think I think I'm doing?*" Jake had countered.

At this point, P.D. had stopped singing and spoken up.

"*Don' have to ask wha' Jake thinks he's doin', Callie,*" he'd declared in a chiding tone. "*Oughta be ob-vibious. Him 'n' me're havin' fun!*"

Callie made an inarticulate sound of distress and opened her eyes. Fun, P.D. had said. *Fun!*

"What was I supposed to think when I heard that?" she demanded of the almost empty kitchen. There was a whimper from the room's other occupant. Callie glanced down at its source. "Oh, hush up, Buttercup!" she commanded crossly. The pregnant dog flattened herself against the linoleum as best she could and went silent.

Years before—around the time she was five or six—Callie had heard her paternal grandfather announce that he was about to "splavocate" over some political issue. Well, she'd been close to "splavocating" after P.D. had pitched in his two cents' worth. She'd either had to tell Jake Turner exactly what she thought of his drunken, disgraceful behavior or explode.

Yet no sooner had she started giving the man a piece of her mind than he'd begun rejecting every assertion she was making. He'd also had the gall to suggest that she—*she*—was partially to blame for P.D.'s condition! She'd accused. He'd denied. He'd attacked. She'd defended. The situation had quickly escalated into whispered warfare.

Callie had no idea how long she and Jake would have gone on with their sotto voce argument had P.D. not interrupted with the quavery announcement that he thought he was going to be very sick, very soon. She only knew that her half brother's pathetic-sounding words had brought about an immediate cessation of hostilities.

The hour that had followed was, mercifully, a blur. She and Jake had taken turns holding P.D.'s head over the bathroom basin while he did his best to retch up everything he'd ever eaten. They'd mopped the teenager's clammy forehead with damp washcloths, and also assured him that, contrary to his most fervent wishes, he wasn't going to die just yet.

Callie couldn't say for certain what had sparked her suspicion that she'd made a mistake when she'd accused Jake of being drunk. Maybe it had been the sure-footed way he'd navigated the route to the bathroom. Maybe it had been the deftness of his hands as he'd cared for P.D. Then again, maybe it had been the look in his eye when he'd told her she could either pitch in and help or get the hell out of the way.

In any case, suspicion had quickly solidified into certainty. It had become crystal clear to Callie that Jake Turner was not inebriated. He might reek of alcohol, but he was as sober as a preacher on Sunday.

And once Callie had accepted that her initial assessment of Jake's condition had been totally wrong, she'd had to start questioning her assumptions about his responsibility for P.D.'s outrageous behavior as well. She'd soon come to the inescapable conclusion that she'd been guilty of a gigantic error in judgment.

Callie sighed heavily and added some buttermilk to the ingredients in the bowl. Putting the fork she'd been using aside, she began to knead the mixture with her hands.

She didn't have to close her eyes to recall what had happened next. The memory of it was burned into very cell of her body and brain.

"Callie?" P.D. had said weakly when she'd turned to leave his bedside. Jake had already moved away and was standing in the doorway.

"Yes, P.D.?" she'd responded immediately, pivoting back.

"Don' be...don' be mad at Jake, 'kay?" the teenager had pleaded drowsily. *"Not his...fault, Callie. He din' do...din' do...nothin'. So don' go bein'...mad...at him-m-mmmmm..."*

Callie had leaned over and gently stroked P.D.'s brow. Her fingers had been less than steady. She'd straightened after a moment, desperately trying to disguise the inner turmoil she was experiencing. She'd been acutely conscious that Jake was scrutinizing every move she made. Her entire nervous system had quivered with the knowledge.

She'd approached Jake slowly, her mind registering all kinds of details about his appearance. The mussed-up state of his thick, tawny hair. The challenging set of his angular features. The provocative thumbs-through-belt-loops stance he'd assumed.

Callie had felt uncertain. Embarrassed. Ashamed. Her heart had been pounding. The unjustified accusations she'd made had reverberated in her skull. They'd gotten louder with each step she'd taken.

She'd seen a dangerous flash of anger in Jake's blue-green eyes when she'd come to a halt about two feet away from him. She'd expected that. Heaven knew, he'd had every right in the world to be furious about the things she'd said and done. If their places had been reversed, she would have been utterly outraged.

But there'd been something in Jake's compelling eyes that was even more potent than anger. Something Callie hadn't expected and couldn't immediately identify. Something that had caused the rhythm of her pulse to alter and accelerate the instant she caught a glimpse of it.

Callie hadn't understood what this "something" was until Jake's gaze had flicked downward for a second then rebounded to her face. It had been then—and only then—that she'd become aware of what she was wearing. Or, rather, of what she *wasn't* wearing.

She'd glanced down at herself and been shocked to see that the upper half of the sleeveless white nightgown she had on had been rendered virtually transparent by splotches of water. The damp fabric of the scoop-necked bodice had clung to her like a second skin, clearly revealing the pale curves of her breasts and the pouting pinkness of their tips.

Callie had felt—had seen—her nipples go taut. The sudden tightening had triggered a white-hot tremor lower down in her body. Her heart had skipped a beat and her throat had closed up. She'd swayed just a little.

She'd started to whisper Jake's name on a shaky breath only to break off, gasping, when he caught her by her upper arms. The press of his work-callused fingertips into her soft flesh had stopped just short of causing pain.

"I've only got one thing to say to you, Callie," he'd told her in a harsh undertone. *"And that one thing is—if people jumped off cliffs the way you jump to conclusions, the human race would have one hell of a problem!"*

"I—I'm s-sorry—" she'd stammered, trying to still the sudden trembling of her body.

"I don't want your damned apology!"

And then there'd been a wild, wanton instant when Callie had thought Jake was going to kiss her. One truly heart-stopping split second in time when she'd *wanted* him to pull her hard against him and claim her mouth with his own. She'd felt her body and brain fill with a hot, honeyed mix of anticipation and apprehension that had the force of two weeks' worth of unadmitted yearning behind it. Her lips had quivered, parted and she'd heard herself make a pleading sound deep in her throat.

But Jake hadn't kissed her. His fingers had tightened on her arms for a moment and his head had even started to dip. Then he'd stopped, his features going rigid with what had looked like shock. An expression she couldn't begin to put a name to had blazed up in his eyes only to be ruthlessly extinguished.

He'd said something under his breath that Callie had been too stunned to understand. Her name perhaps. Or a curse. Then he'd opened his hands and released her so abruptly she'd nearly toppled over. Before she'd had a chance to recover, he'd spun on his heel and strode off down the hall to his room.

She'd shuddered when she'd heard the sound of his door shutting behind him. The sound hadn't been a slam. In fact, Jake had closed the door with a barely audible click. But the frustrating finality of that tiny—

"Uh...Callie?"

Callie came back to the present with a jolt. Reality hit her like a bucket of ice water. She turned away from the counter, heart hammering, face flushed, fingers sticky with buttermilk biscuit dough.

"P.D.!" she managed to get out.

Her half brother was standing about six feet away. He was clad in a ratty flannel bathrobe and listing slightly to the left. "Are you all right?" he questioned, peering at her with bloodshot eyes.

"What?"

"You were makin' some real funny noises when I came in."

"M-me?" Callie wiped her hands against the apron she had on and manufactured a laugh. She wondered whether her cheeks looked as hot as they felt. "I'm fine, P.D. Just fine. Uh—what about you?"

It was probably as good a gauge of P.D.'s post-binge befuddlement as any that he accepted her assurances. Instead of pressing the issue of what she'd been doing when he'd come in, he wrinkled his brow, apparently pondering her question about his own condition.

"I think I better sit down," he finally announced.

Callie watched him shuffle slowly to the kitchen table and gingerly lower himself into a chair. He looked awful. His complexion was pasty and there were purple-gray circles beneath his eyes. Half his hair seemed to have been glued flat to his skull. The other half was sticking out in tufts.

"Pretty bad, huh?" P.D. asked after a few moments.

"Pretty bad," Callie agreed.

He rubbed the knuckles of his right hand across his obviously aching brow, then glanced aimlessly around the kitchen. Eventually his eyes sought Callie's once again.

"Is Aunt Henny here?"

"She's at church. She's going to have Sunday dinner with her friend, Petal Conroy."

"Does she...uh...know?" he asked hesitantly, clearly miserable at the possibility she might.

"Aunt Henny has no idea what happened," Callie responded. She paused, considering what she needed to say next. She'd done a great deal of soul-searching about what had happened the night before. While her feelings about the episode were still confused, she'd come to a few decisions about what tack she was going to take with P.D.

"Aunt Henny doesn't know *anything?*"

Callie shook her head. "She doesn't know anything," she reiterated. "And I, for one, don't intend to change that."

It took P.D. a few moments to process this last statement. "You mean you're not going to tell her what I did?" he questioned in an astonished tone.

"I'm going to keep quiet for her sake, P.D.," Callie said sternly. "Not yours."

The teenager nodded his understanding, then dropped his chin into his chest and began fiddling with the belt of his bathrobe. He blinked rapidly several times. His Adam's apple bobbed up and down as though he was trying to swallow a lump in his throat.

"I'm sorry, C-Callie," he said finally, his voice tremulous. "I'm really, truly, sincerely sorry."

Callie sighed. After a moment, she crossed to the kitchen table and sat down in the chair opposite her half brother. "I know you are, P.D."

"I just got so mad..." He gestured expressively.

"I know."

P.D. went back to plucking at his bathrobe. "Are you goin' to punish me?"

Callie was surprised to find herself fighting back a smile. "I think you're doing a fine job of punishing yourself, P.D.," she answered truthfully.

The teenager brought his head up with a jerk, then winced at the suddenness of the movement. "Yeah," he concurred faintly.

"Can I get you anything?" she asked. Although she didn't doubt that enduring what appeared to be the hangover from hell would do her half brother some good, she hated to see him suffering.

P.D. gave her a wan smile. "No, that's okay. I took some aspirins before I came down. They should kick in pretty soon."

There was a brief silence. Buttercup waddled across the linoleum floor and started snuffling around Callie's feet. The dog's movements were even more awkward than usual. She was barely two weeks from delivery.

"Uh, Callie... about me bein', uh, drunk last night—" P.D. eventually began.

"I know what happened," she interrupted.

Her half brother shook his head vehemently, then groaned. He took a second to recover, then pressed ahead determinedly. "Look, I know you think Jake took me out and got me—"

"I *know* what happened, P.D.," Callie repeated, acutely conscious of the way her pulse jumped at the very mention of Jake Turner's name. "You see, I heard from Seth Avery's mother this morning."

While P.D. had undoubtedly killed a few brain cells the previous evening, he hadn't suffered any serious diminution of intellect. It was obvious from his expression that he understood exactly what Callie's words implied.

"Miz—Miz Avery called here?" he asked apprehensively.

Callie nodded. If she'd harbored any residual inclination toward blaming Jake for P.D.'s drunkenness, it had been obliterated by the irate phone call she'd received from Donna Avery about an hour before. The mother of P.D.'s best buddy had made it absolutely clear who'd been responsible for what.

"She thought I should know that Seth's daddy caught him trying to crawl in through his bedroom window just after midnight last night."

P.D. gulped. "Really?"

"Mmm, hmm. He thought Seth was a burglar. He almost shot him."

It was hard to imagine P.D. turning any paler than he already was, but he managed it. "Sh-shot—?"

"Mrs. Avery seems to feel that shooting Seth might have been a kindness, given his condition."

P.D. groaned his comprehension.

"According to her, Seth and three or four of his friends snuck off to Flat Rock Pond last night for a little drinking party," Callie continued calmly. "She says last night wasn't the first time they'd done such a thing."

P.D. looked stricken. "I only snuck out once before," he confessed in a rush. "I swear. Cross my heart and hope to die. I *swear*. Only once before. It was back in June, right after school let out. But I'll never do it again. I promise. Never again." He paused to draw breath, then asked anxiously, "You—you believe me, don't you, Callie?"

Callie considered the matter, then nodded. "Yes, P.D.," she said slowly. "I believe I do."

They spent time talking more frankly than they had in many months. Eventually—inevitably—P.D. brought up Jake Turner's name once more. Callie did what she thought was a subtle job of redirecting the conversation. But less than a minute later, she found herself deflecting another mention of the man. And, less than thirty seconds after that, she had to do the same thing all over again.

"P.D.—" she finally began, recognizing that she couldn't keep evading the issue.

The teenager overrode her. "Callie, why don't you like Jake?" he asked bluntly.

Callie's heart lurched. "Why—what—I never said—" she stammered.

"He likes you."

These three short syllables momentarily deprived Callie of the ability to speak. Whatever Jake Turner felt toward her—and, after the previous night it was obvious he felt *something*—she seriously doubted it involved any form of "liking."

"At least I think he does," the teenager amended reflectively, dragging the frayed cuff of his bathrobe under his nose. "I mean, he's always askin' questions about you."

"Questions?" Callie croaked.

"He told me I should be more considerate of your feelin's, too," P.D. went on, apparently oblivious to the welter of conflicting emotions he'd unleashed within his half sister. "He gave me heck for leavin' that rub—" He broke off abruptly, his previously pale cheeks flaming red.

"He—" Callie paused, swallowing hard. She knew she couldn't avoid referring to Jake by name. It would be too revealing. "Jake told you what I found in your jeans last weekend?"

P.D. inclined his head in cautious confirmation, his eyes guarded.

Callie registered the teenager's wariness with a pang. She should have spoken to him about the condom and she knew it. But she hadn't been able to find the right moment, the right words. It was galling to think that Jake had taken on the responsibility she'd shirked. It made her feel even worse about the injustice she'd done him.

"Did he tell you anything else, P.D.?" she asked after a moment.

"Just that you were upset. Which I guess I can understand. Only it's not—uh, well—uh—" P.D. grimaced, the color in his cheeks still high. "Oh, heck, Callie! It's not like I'm actually *doin'* anythin'. I just don't want anybody to think I'm a—a—well, you know. But, I'm not doin' anythin'. I mean, I don't even have a steady girl yet." He gave her a very direct look. "You don't think I'd go out and do it with just *anybody,* do you?"

Callie regarded her half brother for several seconds, silently admitting that Jake Turner had been right about a great many things. P.D. was not a kid anymore. The ten-year-old boy she'd once hugged and soothed had grown into a young man right before her eyes. Yet, as deeply as she loved him, as carefully as she'd tried to care for him, she'd refused to acknowledge the transformation until this moment. She couldn't condone what he'd done the night before, but she was finally beginning to comprehend the feelings of frustration that had driven him to do it.

"To tell the truth, P.D.," she said quietly, "I never really thought about you 'doing it' at all until last weekend."

The teenager's eyes widened. "You think there's somethin' wrong with me?" he asked in an alarmed tone.

"No, no!" Callie assured him quickly. She was definitely going to have to keep reminding herself about the fragility of the adolescent male ego. "I think things are very right with you. But . . . well, let's just say I'm going to need a little time to get used to the idea of what your being sixteen really means—okay?"

P.D. smiled crookedly. "Okay."

Callie turned her head and looked out the kitchen windows. The reality of her half brother's maturation wasn't the only idea she had to get used to, she reflected. There was the matter of her monumental error in judgment, too.

The kitchen windows faced west. Callie knew Quarter Oaks lay to the west, not too many miles from where she was sitting. And Quarter Oaks, according to the two-sentence note she'd found taped to the refrigerator when she'd come downstairs shortly after 8:00 a.m., was where Jake Turner was right now.

The second sentence of that note read: "I'm sorry about last night."

"Callie, what are you thinkin'?" P.D. asked, sounding concerned.

Lips that had almost been kissed the night before curved into a slow smile. "I'm thinking I owe Jake Turner an apology."

Callie and Jake came to terms—temporarily—on a blanket spread beneath one of the great old trees that had given Quarter Oaks its name.

"I'm glad you're here," Jake said, breaking the companionable silence that had fallen between them a few minutes before. While he and Callie had suffered through many awkwardnesses so far, this encounter had proven to be much easier than he'd expected. Of course the most difficult subject had not yet been broached.

Callie smiled at him. She was leaning against the oak's sturdy trunk. He was stretched out a little to her right, lazing with the indolent grace of a jungle cat.

"You're glad now that I've fed you, you mean," she returned, teasing. Much of their conversation of the last hour had been laced with laughter. This had surprised her at first, but she'd quickly come to enjoy the banter. "You certainly didn't seem glad at first."

Jake discarded the drumstick he'd been gnawing on. "I was surprised."

"I didn't mean to startle you. The security guard at the gate said you were the only person on the site. I tried knocking and calling your name, but you obviously didn't hear. So, since the door was unlocked, I let myself in—"

"And followed the sound of me swearing at a piece of mahogany molding." He winced inwardly, remembering his feelings when he'd realized that he'd come within a fraction of an inch of making an irreparable gouge in a virtually flawless length of wood.

"You did seem to be doing a good job of abusing it."

"That was the only good job I did today, believe me." A woodworker needed control, and his usual supply of it had been totally absent earlier. He'd reached the point where he'd decided that the only way he'd recover it was to have his brain rewired to short-circuit all thoughts of Callie Barn-

well. He'd also contemplated having some work done on
another part of his anatomy. An achingly insistent part that
didn't think, just throbbed.

"Mind on other matters?"

Jake gave her a rueful grin, teeth flashing white against
tanned skin. The light stubbling of beard on his chin and
jaw caught the afternoon sun for an instant. To Callie, it
looked as though the lower half of his face had been brushed
with gold dust.

"Oh, yes," he said feelingly, and reached for another
piece of chicken.

Callie had arrived at the one-time home of the Barnwells
of Deacon's Crossing armed with more than a sincere apology. She'd come carrying lunch as well. Before she'd left her
house—and after she'd redone her hair twice and changed
her clothes three times—she'd stuffed a picnic basket full of
the goodies she'd prepared for Sunday dinner.

She'd intended the basket as a peace offering and that was
how it had been accepted. Not without a certain degree of
reluctance, to be sure. But in the end, fried chicken and po-
tato salad had proven to be at least as effective as an olive
branch—and a lot more palatable.

"More biscuits, Mr. Turner?" she inquired, picking up a
laden paper plate and extending it.

"I've had four already, thank you, Miss Barnwell," Jake
replied.

Callie took one herself and nibbled on the edge of it,
thinking back to the start of this encounter. She'd stepped
into the front hallway of the Greek-Revival-style mansion
cautiously, feeling like a trespasser. As she'd opened her
mouth to call Jake's name, she'd heard him cursing from
somewhere in the rear of the house.

As he'd suggested, she'd followed the sound and found
him in a spacious room that was in the process of being
paneled. Again, she'd opened her mouth to speak his name.
But before she could get the word out, he'd stiffened and
turned as though he'd sensed her presence. The emotions
that had sleeted across his strong-featured face in the first

few seconds had come and gone too quickly for her to sort out.

"Were you really surprised to see me, Jake?" Callie asked.

"After last night?" he returned. "Yes."

"Didn't you think I'd want to apologize?"

Jake levered himself into a sitting position, the muscles of his upper arms and torso rippling smoothly. He'd had a blue chambray shirt on earlier. He'd shed it along with his battered work shoes and a heavy leather tool belt when they'd sat down for their picnic.

"I thought we'd gone over this, Callie," he said, putting down the piece of chicken he'd picked up several minutes before and wiping his fingers against his jeans. The scene in the downstairs hall was a closed issue as far as he was concerned. It was what had occurred upstairs in the doorway of P.D.'s bedroom that still had to be dealt with.

"We have," Callie conceded. "But I still feel awful about accusing you—"

"Hey," he interrupted, leaning forward. He pressed a silencing fingertip lightly against her lips, breaking the contact when he felt a small tremor of response. "I've been accused of a lot worse, Callie. I've been guilty of it, too."

Callie shifted, her mouth tingling pleasurably in the wake of Jake's brief touch. She was very conscious of his physical proximity. It made her edgy, but not uncomfortable. In a way her awareness of his body heightened her awareness of her own. The shift of her hair against the back of her neck seemed silkier than usual. The warmth of the sun on her skin felt more sensuous. She even found herself noticing the weight and texture of her clothing each time she moved.

"I'll bet you never corrupted any sixteen-year-olds," she remarked, recalling one of the truly nasty things she'd flung at him.

"Just myself," Jake assured her, then cocked a brow. "Although, there *was* this cheerleader named Bambi Lynn..." He paused provocatively, then continued, "But I seem to remember you telling me you didn't want to hear a single syllable about my sordid affairs.''

It took Callie a moment to place the reference. The memory of their confrontation in the kitchen and the item that had precipitated it brought a stain of hot color to her cheeks. "P.D. told me you told him about that," she said. "I mean, about my finding..." Gesturing awkwardly, she let her voice trail off.

"Does that bother you?"

"Somebody needed to talk to him about it," Callie answered. "It should have been me, but I didn't have the...the..." She grimaced, the list of her sisterly deficiencies too long to narrow to just one.

It bothered Jake to see Callie berating herself. Yes, she'd made a few mistakes in handling her half brother, but he had a hunch those mistakes wouldn't be made again. Mistakes aside, didn't she realize how much she'd given P.D.? Didn't she have any idea of the kind of loving warmth she radiated?

"You didn't have the right equipment?" he suggested with deliberate outrageousness.

"Jake!" Callie gasped.

He masked his satisfaction with his ploy by feigning contrition. "Sorry."

"No, you're not."

He shrugged.

Callie shook her head. "Honestly, I don't know what to do with you."

It was an opening and Jake took it.

"Well, Callie, that makes two of us."

The change in his voice was subtle, but Callie heard it. The shift in his features was slight, but she saw it. Her heartbeat quickened. She felt a prickle of warning run up her spine.

"What?" she asked, trying to maintain a casual tone. "You don't know what to do with you, either?"

Jake registered the sudden wariness in her gray-green eyes. He watched her lift her chin up in a mannerism that had become very familiar to him during the past two weeks.

"No," he answered levelly. "I don't know what to do with you."

Callie's eyes widened. Her nostrils flared on a sharp exhalation of breath. "And what makes you think you have to *do* anythin'?" The strengthening of her Southern accent betrayed her agitation as surely as the rapid pulse at the base of her slender throat.

"What happened last night in P.D.'s bedroom."

A liquid rush of warmth suffused Callie's body. "Nothin' happened," she denied throatily.

Jake shook his head. "Don't be coy, Callie. You and I have been striking sparks off each other for two weeks, and last night we came this close—" He held up his right hand, thumb and index finger barely a hair's-breadth apart. "*This close* to starting a major fire."

Callie swallowed hard, searching his angular features one by one, trying to make sense of what he was saying. Confusion made her confrontational. "Is that why you didn't kiss me last night?" she asked baldly.

Now that he'd begun, Jake didn't know if he was going to be able to finish. But he had to make her understand their situation. Hell, he had to make himself understand it!

"You're not my type, Callie," he said, driven to repeating the phrase that had become his mantra during the previous night.

Callie almost choked. "What—what makes you think I thought I was?" she demanded, her eyes flashing with indignant fury. "What makes you think I'd ever want to be? And if you for one single solitary second flatter yourself that you're *my* type—"

"I don't, dammit!" Jake interrupted harshly. Unable to stop himself, he caught Callie by the upper arms much as he had the night before. She was wearing an off-the-shoulder blouse, so what he took hold of was smooth flesh and satin-textured skin. "That's just the point! You and I are two entirely different kinds of people, Callie. You're hello. I'm goodbye. You're rooted in this town. I've got a two-month lease. There's no way things could work out between us."

Callie tried to jerk away. His fingers tightened to prevent her. "Let me go!" she demanded.

"No! Don't you understand?"

"I understand you're crazy! Now, let go of me!"

"Not until I'm through with you! Callie...Callie, I know all our differences. I know you're not my type and I'm not yours. I knew it from the moment we met. But that didn't stop me from wanting to kiss you in that self-same moment. And it's not *going* to stop me from wanting to kiss you—"

"Well, why don't you just get it over with, then?" Callie challenged, goaded far beyond the limits of common sense.

And so he did.

Hard.

Hot.

Hungry.

Those words barely hinted at the intensity of the kiss Jake gave Callie. She struggled against the devouring, demanding force of it for a second, then surrendered to the wild surge of response that rushed up from the very core of her being. A wave of wanting washed over her, scalding her senses and sweeping away the barriers she'd spent the previous two weeks constructing.

Somehow they'd both knelt up on the picnic blanket. Their bodies were mated from thigh to mouth. Callie moved against Jake restlessly, the shift of her hips urgent beneath the fabric of her skirt. She clutched at him, feeling the convulsive ripple and release of his muscles. She didn't simply yield to the sinuous search of his tongue, she invited it.

Jake lifted one of his hands and fisted it in the soft tangle of her cinnamon silk hair. He tugged on the shoulder-length strands a little, tilting her head back...back...then further back still. Callie moaned deep in her throat when he took ruthless, ravishing advantage of the additional access to her mouth this offered him. She heard herself moan again when she felt his other hand glide down the length of her spine and mold itself to the curve of her bottom.

She arched in answer to this caress, fitting herself against him even more intimately. Her hands came up to lock behind his corded neck. The delicate bite of her nails sent a fiery shiver running down Jake's back. He felt her fingers tangle tightly in his hair.

Jake deepened the kiss, laying claim to the soft interior of Callie's trembling mouth with delving sweeps of his tongue. Her own tongue moved in gliding counterpoint to his. Her fingers spasmed, clenching at the back of his head with almost painful force.

Jake heard himself groan. The blood in his veins was hot. The flesh it nourished hard.

He murmured Callie's name against her lips, then nuzzled a slow, searing path to her throat. Her head fell back as he slid his mouth downward to mark the place where her pulse beat out an unmistakable message of excitement. He licked the skin over the spot, savoring the sudden acceleration he detected.

Jake moved his hands again. His fingertips grazed the elasticized neckline of her blouse, easing it downward. He cupped Callie's delicately rounded breasts. Her nipples went taut against the thin fabric of the garment, pressing into the centers of his palms.

Callie gave a soft cry. Her warm breath fanned Jake's skin with a feather-light mist. Her hands flowed down from his broad shoulders and pressed against the bare skin of his torso. Her fingers winnowed slowly through the rough silk of his chest hair.

Their lips met in a languid, luxurious reunion. Callie's mouth was all sweet, seductive heat. He repaid each one of the pleasures she gave him tenfold, sending honeyed ribbons of heat streaming through her pliant body.

And then . . .

And then it was over.

They eased back, broke apart. The distance between them went from nothing to inches to nearly a foot. Both of them were trembling. Callie's pupils were dilated, her cheeks were pink, her breath was coming in and out in shallow little snatches. Jake's eyes had darkened to midnight-moss, his skin was flushed, and he had to struggle to draw oxygen into his lungs.

Callie crossed her arms in front of her, tugging at the neckline of her blouse. Her chin went up. "Y-you're still n-not my type," she got out.

If Jake had had the breath, he might have laughed. Instead, he said, "I know, Callie. God help both of us, I know."

Six

Callie sighed with relief as she inserted the last of some five dozen straight pins into the hem of the pink chiffon gown she was fitting on the fidgetiest—and most flat-chested—would-be beauty queen she'd ever run into. Sitting back on her heels, she raised her gaze slowly up Stella Avery's lathe-thin body.

"Can I look now?" the milk-pale blonde asked anxiously. She peered down at Callie with big blue eyes. The expression in them reminded Callie of the portrait of a pleading orphan she'd once seen painted on black velvet.

"Yes, Stella," she said, gesturing to the full-length mirror behind the girl. "You can look now."

Stella pirouetted around, nearly losing her balance in the process.

"Watch it!" Callie gasped, envisioning disaster. She surged up from her knees, offering a steadying hand. Stella was probably the sweetest young woman in Deacon's Crossing, which was one of the reasons Callie was willing to work after hours on the creation of her gown for the Miss

Founders' Day Festival pageant. Unfortunately the nine-teen-year-old was also a total klutz.

"It's all right. It's all right," Stella said, regaining her equilibrium. She looked over her shoulder and gave Callie an endearing smile. "I'm still havin' a little problem with these new heels of mine."

"Just be careful," Callie advised, sinking back down into her original position. She slipped a hand around to the small of her back and tried to massage out the knot of tension there.

Stella turned to-and-fro in front of the mirror, studying her reflection from different angles. Callie watched the blue eyes track up and down, then saw the young woman's nearly invisible brows come together in a frown.

"What's wrong, Stella?" Callie had a very strong suspicion of what the problem was.

Stella heaved a gusty sigh. "Well, it's just a beautiful gown," she said sincerely. "You were exactly right about this color and material. It's so much better than that tacky turquoise taffeta I begged you to make up. I mean, this royal rose truly flatters my skin tone. And the chiffon is so floaty and graceful." She fanned open the gown's overskirt to underscore her assertion, then gave a little cry of dismay as five or six pins went flying out. "Oh, Callie, Callie, I'm so sorry!"

"Never mind, Stella," Callie responded patiently. "Just tell me what's bothering you."

Stella jitterbugged around for a few seconds, then smoothed her hand down her front. "I'm just so flat, Callie. I swear, I'd die happy if I had *one-quarter* of what Janie Mae Winslow has!"

Callie rose to her feet, trying not to smile. "Wouldn't that be a little bit of a waste?"

Stella looked blank.

"To have a quarter of what Janie Mae Winslow has and be dead," Callie explained. She glanced at her wristwatch and felt a niggle of disappointment. It was nearly half past six. Jake hadn't promised he was going to come by, she reminded herself firmly. But still . . .

The blonde suddenly started to giggle. "Oh, Callie. You're so funny. I bet you could be on TV."

"I'm sure *The Tonight Show* will be calling any day." Callie cocked her head, searching for the right words to bolster Stella's confidence. She knew the young woman yearned for a voluptuous figure, but it was an impossible dream. While Callie had done what she could with underwires, tucks and some discreet padding, it was a little like trying to transform two anthills into the Alps.

"Last night Seth said I was going to look like a pink popsicle stick on stage at the pageant," Stella reported plaintively, returning to her original theme.

"Your brother's taste is in his mouth when it comes to clothes," Callie countered firmly, maligning P.D.'s best friend without a qualm. "He couldn't match a pair of plaid socks if they came with directions. I think you look very elegant, Stella. And you have a very fashionable figure. There are New York designers who'd kill to fit clothes on a model like you."

Stella puffed up like a dried sponge dropped into water. "Really? Then you don't think I should try maskin' tape?"

Callie checked her watch again. "What?" she asked, more sharply than she'd intended. What if something had happened to him? she worried.

"You know, Callie. *Maskin' tape.* Janie Mae Winslow says there's this cross-your-heart trick you can do with it to get cleavage."

Callie rolled her eyes. "Forget the masking tape, Stella. Please. And stop paying attention to Janie Mae Winslow. I realize she's got more crowns than the Queen of England at this point, but some of her beauty pageant advice is positively bizarre."

Stella's blue eyes widened. "Do you truly think so? Bizarre? Do you know, I *did* think it was kind of disgustin' soundin' when she told me to rub petroleum jelly on my teeth so my lips would slide into a nice, wide smile for the judges. And just the other day she confided to me that she uses hemorrhoid cream to reduce unsightly puffiness under her—''

Callie was saved from learning the location of Janie Mae's unsightly puffiness by the sound of someone rapping boldly on the door of her shop. Stella froze like a fawn caught in the headlights of an oncoming truck.

"Callie?" Jake's resonant male voice called.

Callie's pulse kicked and picked up its previously very steady pace.

"Who do you think—?" the blonde asked anxiously.

"It's a friend, Stella," Callie answered reassuringly, then headed for the front of the store. She smoothed back her hair as she went.

Five days had passed since she and Jake had kissed with such incendiary abandon beneath one of the majestic trees of Quarter Oaks. Just five short days. Less than one week. But what an incredible change their relationship had undergone in that brief period. *"Friend"* was about the last thing she'd ever expected to call Jake Turner, yet a friend was what he'd become.

Not the most comfortable of friends, to be sure. He still went out of his way to needle her every now and again. And she was not above getting after him about one thing or another. There was no denying that the "spark" striking he'd spoken of continued to generate a fair amount of heat between them, either. But they'd reached an accommodation—no, they'd reached an *understanding*—rooted in the very differences Jake had sworn must keep them apart. To put it simply they'd acknowledged a mutual attraction while agreeing it would be unwise to act on it.

He wasn't her type. Jake was going to be leaving Deacon's Crossing before Labor Day.

She wasn't his type. Callie was going to be staying for many, many Labor Days to come.

But that didn't mean they couldn't get along. That didn't mean they couldn't like each other.

"I'm late. I'm sorry," Jake said as soon as Callie unlocked and opened the door for him. He gave her a placating grin which crinkled the skin at the outer corners of his eyes, then flicked a finger beneath her chin. Teasing touches—casual caresses—had become the norm in their new relationship.

"No problem," she responded, noting that he was wearing his usual T-shirt and jeans. He definitely did more for white cotton knit and wash-faded denim than any man of her acquaintance. "We didn't sign a contract."

"Right," Jake agreed, ambling into the shop. He got a brief whiff of Callie's cologne as he moved by her. She wore a faint, floral scent that managed to be both fresh and a little old-fashioned. He thought it suited her perfectly. "I've got the material for your storeroom shelves in the pickup. The local hardware store didn't have the brackets I wanted, so I take a run to—" He broke off, suddenly realizing there was a third person present. "Oh. I didn't know you had a customer."

Callie's eyes shifted from Jake's polite face to Stella's pale one. The not-so-budding beauty pageant contestant was exhibiting something less than princessly poise. To put it bluntly, she looked as though she'd just been poleaxed.

Callie suppressed a sigh. She understood how Stella felt, but she wished the nineteen-year-old wouldn't be so obvious about it. While Jake had been tolerant of the fact that her clerk, Sage Bolling, trailed him like a puppy dog every time he came into Callie's Corner, she knew he wasn't comfortable with such attention.

"Jake," she said, "this is Miss Stella Avery. Stella, this is Mr. Jake Turner."

"The man who's livin' with you, right?" Stella asked, floating forward. Her moment of grace came to an ungainly end when she caught the heel of her right shoe in her hem and nearly took a header into a rack of clothes.

Jake and Callie moved in unison to help the hapless young woman.

"Easy, easy," Jake said.

"Are you okay?" Callie asked anxiously, making a swift inspection of the gown as she helped steady the blonde. No major rips or tears, thank heaven.

"Oh, I'm fine," Stella asserted breathlessly. "It's just these new high heels." She threw Jake an apologetic look. "I have weak ankles?"

Jake didn't quite understand the young woman's shift to a questioning inflection, but he sensed he was supposed to make some reply. "A lot of people have that problem," he declared.

Stella made a swoony little sound. "Y'all are *so* understandin'."

Lord, Callie thought, this is worse than Sage Bolling!

"Stella's one of the contestants in this year's Miss Founders' Day pageant," she said.

"Really?" Jake gave Callie a quick smile, his blue-green eyes amused.

"This is my first time enterin' a beauty contest," Stella elaborated. "My on-stage talent's goin' to be stuffin'."

Jake caught a warning look from Callie and transformed a chuckle of disbelief into a cough. "Stuffing?" he echoed carefully.

"Cooking," Callie clarified. She could tell what Jake was thinking. Honestly, the man should be ashamed of having such a dirty mind.

"That's right," Stella affirmed happily, then shifted into the interrogatory again. "I'm doin' a lightnin' fast preparation of a Thanksgivin' feast? Includin' stuffin' a turkey? While doin' this original dramatic recitation about the importance of good nutrition?"

"Oh, I see." Jake was relieved. "Well, I'm sorry I'll miss it."

"Miss it? Y'all won't be here?"

"Jake's leaving at the end of August," Callie said, trying not to dwell on the fact that this was only a little more than five weeks away.

Stella looked crushed. "Then he'll miss your presentation, too, Callie."

Jake turned to Callie, brows raised. He knew she'd gotten a kick out of his reaction to Stella's stuffing. Maybe this was an opportunity for some quid pro quo. "You're in the pageant?"

"Oh, no," Stella rushed in. "She's part of the historical tableaux and readin's? She does excerpts from her Great-great-great-great-aunt Caroline Anne's diaries?" She glanced at Callie. "I cried real tears last year when you read that white lace promises part, Callie. It was the most touchin' thing I ever heard."

"Thank you, Stella," Callie said, a bit embarrassed. "Look, why don't you go change your clothes. I'm sure your family's expecting you."

"Oh, all right," the blonde assented immediately. She glanced at Jake. "I'll be right back?"

Jake nodded. He waited until Stella had disappeared into one of the small dressing rooms before asking Callie in an undertone, "Why was she making everything into a question when she spoke to me?"

Callie smothered a laugh. "Because she's a woman and you're a man and a woman is supposed to defer to a man's superior opinion."

His sensually-shaped mouth twisted. "Then how come the only question I hear from you is 'And what the hell is that supposed to mean, Jake Turner?'"

"I do not use profanity, sir!" Callie disputed, feigning an ultra-genteel shudder of shock.

"You don't defer, either."

"The day your opinion is superior to mine, I will."

"Uh-huh. And in the meantime, I can go screw shelf brackets, right?"

Callie poked him, trying not to laugh. "Don't be tacky."

Jake trapped her hand and interlaced their fingers. He brushed aside a thought about how comfortably Callie's palm fitted against his. "Watch it," he warned. "You don't want to start anything you can't handle. I've got six inches and at least seventy pounds on you, lady."

"The bigger they are, the harder they fall," Callie riposted a bit breathlessly. The press of Jake's work-hardened hand sent tiny jolts of electricity arrowing up her arm.

"Just be careful I don't fall on—"

"Callie?" It was a wail of distress. "Oh, Callie, I think I've done somethin' just *awful* to the zipper on this gown!"

It took Callie about ten minutes to extract Stella from her gown, get her into her street clothes, and gently shepherd her out the door. During that time Jake carried in the material for the shelves he intended to put up. He and Stella had another brief chat before she left. Recalling a towheaded toothpick of a teenager P.D. had introduced to him a few days before, Jake asked whether she and Seth Avery were related. This inquiry elicited a reluctant affirmative plus the information that Seth was being threatened with enrollment in a military academy because of his drunken behavior the previous weekend.

Although Callie didn't pay much attention to the conversation, she did see Jake's features tighten for an instant at the mention of Seth's possible exile. She succumbed to curiosity about the brief change of expression after Stella made her exit.

"You don't like military academies, Jake?" she asked.

Jake ran his thumb over the edge of one of the shelves he'd brought, assessing the need to do some sanding. He wasn't really surprised that Callie had picked up on his negative response to what Stella had said. He'd learned the lady could be very perceptive when she chose.

"I attended a couple during my inglorious academic career," he answered with a shrug.

Callie frowned. "I thought you said you went to a prep school."

Jake glanced at her. He'd revealed quite a lot about his background to her during the past few days. Although it was clear his story stirred her compassion—even her anger on his behalf—he detected no pity, for which he was thankful. Pity was something he didn't want or need. He'd built a strong life for himself.

He knew that Callie had done the same. While she'd known family love and security, she'd also endured more than her share of personal tragedies. In response to his confidences, she'd confirmed much of the information he'd already garnered from P.D. Specifically, that she'd lost her mother to cancer when she was eleven and that a car accident thirteen years later had killed her adored stepmother and crippled her father beyond any prayer of recovery. She had said nothing about the fiancé Bernice, the waitress, had mentioned, and Jake hadn't pressed.

"Jake?" Callie prompted.

He picked up the thread of their conversation. "I did go to a couple of prep schools. But after my father died, my mother decided I needed a strong male hand to guide me." He shook his head. "Funny how she didn't notice that I hadn't had one while my father was alive. Anyway one of her many admirers recommended the military school he'd sent his sons to, so off I went."

"You weren't happy?"

"I was hell on wheels. Got thrown out six weeks after I arrived. Same story, different verse, at the next place."

"And then?"

He smiled suddenly. "And then I ended up at a military school with a man named Sam Swayze on the payroll."

"Sam—the man Aunt Henny said called the house the other day from Vermont? Your business partner?" Callie tried not to sound too curious. While Jake had shared a lot about himself with her in recent days, she knew that opening up was not easy for him. Then again, it wasn't always easy for her, either. She'd told him the truth about her experiences of the past six years, but she hadn't told him the whole truth.

Jake nodded. "Sam was the school's handyman. An ex-Marine who made fine furniture in his basement. I met him after I lost my temper and kicked a hole through a door. After he read me the riot act, he made me help fix the damned thing."

"And that's how you started woodworking," Callie concluded softly.

"That's how I started woodworking," Jake agreed. "Now, let's get started on *this* little woodworking project, okay?"

Callie watched him pull the bottom of his T-shirt out of his jeans and start to peel the garment upward. "Jake—" she began at the point where he'd bared an unsettling amount of tanned, well-toned torso.

He stopped. "What?"

"Don't you keep your shirt on for *anything?*"

Jake surveyed Callie with a wicked gleam in his eyes. "What have you got in mind?"

"So that was the famous Janie Mae Winslow, hmm?" Jake inquired the following Monday as he and Callie strolled toward Earle's All You Can Eat. He'd come to Deacon's Crossing intending to take the lady to lunch, and he hadn't taken *no* for an answer. He had a companionable arm draped over Callie's shoulder, just to make sure she didn't try to reverse course and head back to her shop.

"Yes," Callie confirmed shortly. "That was the famous Janie Mae Winslow."

"Obviously a woman outstanding in her field."

"If you *like* obvious. She gives new meaning to the phrase 'my cup runneth over.'"

Jake chuckled. There was no denying Janie Mae Winslow's brunette and buxom appeal, but he vastly preferred willowy thirty-year-olds with soft brown hair and changeable eyes. "Meee-yow," he teased.

Callie flashed him a quelling glance. "I suppose you enjoyed her bein' all over you like glaze on a doughnut?"

"Do you know you get very Southern-sounding when you're ticked off?"

"I am a Southerner! How else do you expect me to sound?" Callie's hip bumped his. She felt his arm tighten against her shoulder for a split second.

"You're a *lapsed* Southerner."

She rolled her eyes. Now the man was accusing her of being a regional backslider. "And what's that supposed to mean?"

"You spent—what was it you told me?—nearly five years in New York? I'm afraid you carry the taint of Northern exposure, sweetheart."

Something inside Callie trembled a little at the endearment, but she quickly told herself to ignore the foolish response. Jake calling her sweetheart had no more meaning than Bernice, the waitress at Earle's All You Can Eat, calling people sugar.

"I may have when I first got back here, Jake," she responded, then realized with a slight shock of surprise that she *was* drawling more than normal. She decided she might as well pour it on like syrup. "But ah have seen the light and returned to the fold of mah beloved ancestors. Ah am a true daughter of Dixie once mo-ah."

Jake was still laughing at her performance when they settled into the vinyl-covered seats of one of Earle's five booths.

"People are staring at you," Callie informed him repressively.

"People always stare at me when I come in here," he returned. "I'm a celebrity."

"A—what?"

"According to Augustus Bates, I'm the first real man the lovely ladies of the esteemed Barnwell clan have clasped to their bosoms in more than a century." He winked, watching Callie flush. "Excluding blood relatives, of course."

"You've met Augustus Bates?" she inquired stiffly. She was aware that the females of her family didn't have a particularly good history when it came to the opposite sex, but it nettled her to think that their romantic failures had become the stuff of local lore. Then again, she didn't suppose it should surprise her. The residents of Deacon's Crossing thrived on gossip—past and present.

"Why, yes, he has, my dear." This mellifluous affirmation came from behind Callie.

"Mr. Bates," Jake greeted the older man with a nod. He and the bane of Miss Henny's existence had encountered each other several times since their first meeting.

Callie shifted around. "Hello, Mr. Bates," she said with a trace of discomfort.

"Afternoon, Callie. Afternoon, Jake," the newspaperman returned genially. "I do hope you'll excuse my eavesdroppin' and intrudin'. But I heard my name and my curiosity was piqued. A result of my journalistic profession as much as my natural desire to know what people are sayin' about me."

"It was nothing, really," Callie assured him. One of Deacon's Crossing's native sons, Augustus Bates had returned to town roughly a year before after some four decades of newspapering up north. Callie barely knew him. He seemed like a very courtly gentleman. She couldn't help wondering what he'd done to earn her sweet-natured aunt's undying enmity.

"Would you like to sit down?" Jake invited.

"Oh, no, thank you very kindly. I must be on my way. However—I would like to confirm our appointment for next week? I am delighted the people representin' the new owner of Quarter Oaks have finally consented to allow me to do an article about the restoration y'all are performin'. It's no secret that gracious old place went halfway to ruination during the unfortunate five-year probate fight which followed the previous owner's untimely demise. But where there's a will there's a way for money-grubbin' heirs to squabble over it, I suppose. You are undoubtedly aware that people hereabouts are curious about what's bein' done to Quarter Oaks—bein' that the new owner is Japanese and all. But, of course, there is a certain logic to that. After all, the Japanese are renowned for their respect for tradition. And Quarter Oaks is the very essence of tradition, in my humble opinion."

Not for the first time, it occurred to Jake that he'd dearly love to listen in on a conversation between Augustus Bates and Henrietta Barnwell. The combined word count would be astronomical.

"Next Wednesday afternoon still sounds fine, Mr. Bates," he said, harking back to the question that had triggered the older man's lengthy monologue. "I'll give you the grand tour."

"Splendid. I regret not havin' the opportunity to interview the owner himself. But I understand that Mr. Hideo Ichiai is a rather reclusive man, intendin' to remain in Tokyo until the restoration and refurbishin' is entirely completed. I have assured his representatives—the ones from his conglomerate's office in Atlanta?—that I will do nothin' to violate his privacy."

"No pictures, hmm?" Jake deduced.

Augustus Bates smiled. "Well, perhaps one or two. But taken very discreetly." He turned his attention to Callie. "I do apologize for runnin' on like this, my dear. I hope you're not feelin' excluded."

"No, not at all," she said. "It's very interesting. I'm sure the article will be wonderful."

"Perhaps it will even win the approval of your lovely aunt. She's well, I trust?"

"Aunt Henny's fine. Thank you for asking."

"It would be remiss of me not to. It's gratifyin' to hear that Miss Henny is well. Would you be so kind as to give her my regards?"

"Of course, Mr. Bates."

"And please, do assure her that I have no intention of intrudin' on her enjoyment durin' our upcomin' sojourn to our state's fine capital."

It took Callie a moment to figure out what the older man meant. She'd just discovered that morning that her aunt and half brother had travel plans for the following weekend.

"Oh, are you going on the church outing to Atlanta, too?" she asked.

"Indeed I am. May I infer that you will not be takin' advantage of this opportunity?"

Callie glanced across the table at Jake. "No. No, I'm not."

"I see," Mr. Bates said with a nod. "Well, it's no secret you're a very busy young lady, my dear. So many affairs to attend to." He smiled. "Now, I really must be goin'. I leave you to your repast. If I might be so bold to recommend—the ham hocks are particularly succulent today."

And with that, Augustus Bates tipped a hat he didn't have on and strolled away.

"Jake," Callie began in an appalled tone, gazing across the table. One of the words the newspaperman had just uttered was reverberating in her ears. "Jake, you don't think he thinks we're—" She paused, not wanting to say it aloud.

"What? That we're having an affair?" Jake continued the sentence, apparently unfazed by the possibility. "Not at all, Callie. I just think that's the way he talks."

"Well—"

"Hi, Callie sugar. Hi, Jake," Bernice the waitress interrupted. She deposited two glasses of iced tea on the table. "Unsweetened tea, just the way you both like it."

Callie felt her cheeks grow warm. She wondered how much the other woman had overheard.

"Thanks, Bernice," Jake said easily.

"Saw you talkin' to Mr. Bates," the waitress commented. "I s'pose he told you the excitin' news."

"What news?" Callie asked a bit stiffly.

Bernice's brows climbed toward her hairline. "You mean, he didn't? Why, I swear, you'd think he'd be eager to tell you, Callie. Seein' that it concerns you in a way."

"What news?" Callie repeated, staring at the other woman.

The waitress smiled sunnily. " 'Bout Belle Terre. Seems this Eye-choo fella from Japan—the one who's bought it?—is goin' to change the name."

Although most of her attention was focused on Bernice, Callie couldn't help notice that Jake seemed quite indifferent to this conversation. He had his head down, apparently engrossed in the historic illustrations on the paper place mat in front of him.

"Change it, Bernice?" she echoed. "Change it to what?"

"That's why it concerns you. According to Mr. Bates, Eye-choo's goin' to call it Quarter Oaks again. Ain't that somethin'? Your Aunt Henny'll be happier than a kitten on a catnip cloud when she hears, I'll bet." Bernice beamed for a moment, then became businesslike. "Well, I'll just leave you two to decide what you want for lunch. Give me a little shout when you're ready to order. Mr. Bates had the ham hocks. He said they were sucky-something. I know it sounds disgustin', but I think he liked them. I mean, he looked like he would've relished lickin' the plate if his mama hadn't taught him better manners."

Feeling slightly stunned, Callie watched the waitress bustle away. Then she looked across the table at Jake. He was still studying the place mat. There was something odd about the intensity of his scrutiny.

"Jake, did you know about this?" she questioned. "About the name being changed back to Quarter Oaks?"

Jake looked up, silently cursing small towns and their lack of secrets. "I thought as far as you were concerned, it's always been Quarter Oaks," he parried.

"You did know about it, then?"

"I didn't know it was definite." He shrugged and took a sip of iced tea.

Callie frowned, her pleasure over the news dimming in the face of her puzzlement about Jake's behavior. She couldn't believe he was treating this matter so cavalierly. Not that she expected him to jump up and down and make a fool of himself about it. She really couldn't picture him making a fool out of himself about anything. Still, she knew he had some understanding of what the Quarter Oaks name meant to her family. So why was he acting as though this didn't make a bit of difference? Why was he acting as though—

And then Callie thought she understood.

Acting.

Jake's indifference was a pose. He was *acting* as though it was no big deal that Quarter Oaks was going to be known by its true name once again. And he most likely was acting that way because he'd had something to do with the change and he didn't want her to know about it.

Callie had noticed, almost from the very start, that Jake Turner had an aversion to being given credit for doing good deeds. She could think of several occasions when he'd turned downright rude in response to her efforts to express her appreciation of work he'd done around the house. She'd also heard him rebuff—albeit very gently—her aunt's attempts to thank him for his assistance.

There'd been a time she would have put the worst possible interpretation on this behavior. But that time was over.

"It's because of you, isn't it?" she said slowly, holding his eyes with hers. "It's because of you that the new owner's going to change the name back to Quarter Oaks."

Jake shrugged again. He'd expected—hoped, really—that the news about the name wouldn't be announced until after he was long gone from Deacon's Crossing. He'd known that if word got out, it would probably prompt questions he didn't want to deal with. Questions like why he'd bothered to mention Belle Terre's original name to some yuppie from Atlanta in the first place. He still couldn't figure out what had motivated him to do that.

"You did something—said something—" Callie wasn't going to let him off the hook.

Jake rubbed the side of the condensation-fogged iced-tea glass with his finger. "All right. Yeah," he admitted flatly. "I said something about Belle Terre once being called Quarter Oaks to the main supervisor from Atlanta a couple of weeks ago. He apparently passed the word along to Tokyo and Ichiai apparently liked the idea of going back to the original name. That's it. End of story." He went back to examining the place mat.

Callie tilted her head to one side, pondering Jake's effort to deny he'd done anything she—or anyone in her family—should feel beholden for. It was her experience that most people liked having others in their debt. It made her a little sad to see that Jake was absolutely determined to avoid such obligations.

"I'm not your type, Callie," he'd told her. And that was true. Except . . .

Callie reached over and put one of her hands on top of one of his. She felt him stiffen, saw him look up once more.

"You know what I think, Jake Turner?" she asked.

His mouth twisted. "I shudder to guess, Callie Barnwell."

"I think you're a very nice man, but you don't want anyone to know it."

Jake laughed. "Callie," he said when he got his breath back, "I'm a lot of things. But nice ain't one of them."

"You, sir, are a master of your trade," Augustus Bates opined two days later as he and Jake completed their inspection of the first floor of the Quarter Oaks mansion. They'd been accompanied on the tour by Mr. Bates's dog, a purebred basset hound named Beauregard.

"Thank you," Jake said. Bending down, he gave Beauregard a casual scratch between the ears. While he'd never been a pet person, he had to admit that the newspaperman's dog was an appealing animal. Not quite as appealing as Miss Henny's Buttercup, of course. But that was to be expected. Buttercup—like her mistress—was possessed of some very peculiar charms.

"What was the name of that moldin' pattern in the dinin' room?"

"Egg and dart."

"Hand carved, you said."

"That's right."

"But not all by yourself and your partner—what was the name again?"

"Sam Swayze. And no. We didn't do all the carving ourselves. Our workshop in Vermont has a full-time staff of six."

"But you are responsible for that amazin' combination of shelves and cabinets goin' up in the library?"

"That's my design, yes. I did the measuring and prep work when I was down here in April. Then we did most of the construction and carving back at the workshop. Some of the pieces were shipped to Deacon's Crossing. Some I brought with me in my pickup."

"Yes. Yes. I understand you're quite a travelin' man. And you're off to Great Britain once you're done here?"

In a little over a month, Jake reminded himself silently. Then he said aloud, "We've been contacted about a commission for the Earl of Malham. It's a wedding present."

The older man shook his head wonderingly. "Remarkable. Truly remarkable. Do you know, Jake, the magnificence of this restoration effort leaves me almost bereft of speech?" He paused, then queried casually, "Has either of the lovely Barnwell ladies had an opportunity to view this transformation?"

"Callie's had the grand tour," Jake replied. He smiled a little at the memory. Callie's reaction to the mansion had given him a great deal of pleasure. There'd been an almost sensual quality to her appreciation of his work. She'd had to touch everything—to savor with her fingers as well as her eyes.

"Indeed?" Augustus Bates came to a halt. Beauregard hunkered down immediately, the very picture of canine propriety.

Jake hooked his thumbs into his belt loops, conscious that the front of his jeans felt a bit tight. "To tell the truth, I think she was a little reluctant at first. She said something about being the first Barnwell to set foot inside the Quarter Oaks mansion in more than a half century."

"Ah, yes." The newspaperman gave an odd-sounding chuckle. "That would be because of her paternal grandfather. The original Palmer Dean Barnwell. I believe he had some type of political dispute with one of the former owners of this property shortly before World War Two. He swore no Barnwell would ever come near Quarter Oaks again.''

"Sounds serious."

"Oh, that was his style. Palmer Dean Barnwell had political disputes of one kind or another with just about everyone in the county before he got through. He used to fire off letters to the local paper almost daily. My dear departed daddy owned the *Deacon's Crossing Weekly* back then. After receivin' one particularly scathin' epistle, he approached Palmer Dean and asked him whether he was aware that some ravin' lunatic was sendin' out letters signed with his name. I'm afraid my daddy's attempt at levity was not well received."

"Hmm." Jake wondered fleetingly if this story might explain Miss Henny's hostility toward Augustus Bates. It was possible, he supposed. But it was hard for him to picture Callie's aunt nursing a second-generation grudge.

"I take it Miss Henny hasn't been by Quarter Oaks?" Augustus Bates inquired, pausing to flick a bit of sawdust off the lapel of his immaculate white linen suit.

Jake shook his head.

The older man nodded. "I hadn't really expected..." he murmured, glancing around. He seemed to lose himself in thought.

"Would you like to see the second floor now?" Jake asked after a few moments.

Augustus Bates blinked, visibly startled. "Oh...oh, indeed. Please." He snapped his fingers. Beauregard stood instantly, head cocked at a quizzical angle.

Jake gestured toward the stairs. "Things aren't quite as far along up there," he commented. "And the attic's still got to be completely renovated."

"Ah, yes. The attic. Refuge of the sad but saintly Miss Caroline Anne."

Jake checked himself in mid-stride. "What?"

The newspaperman looked surprised. "Why, I'd assumed you must have heard the story by this time. Miss Caroline Anne Barnwell locked herself in the attic on her weddin' day in June of 1875. Or, should I say, what was *meant* to be her weddin' day. Didn't come out for six months. Took her meals from a tray her family left outside the door twice daily. There are those who contend she would have stayed in the attic for the rest of her natural life if the house hadn't been sold out from under her to pay taxes. I personally disagree with such scurrilous assertions. But in any case, Miss Caroline Anne—once the loveliest, most lighthearted of belles—emerged from the attic to become the most devoted doer of good in the history of Deacon's Crossing.''

Jake frowned. It was time to find out exactly what the low-down Yankee bastard he slightly resembled had done, he decided. ''Harriman Gage left Caroline Anne at the altar?''

The newspaperman gestured. ''In a manner of speakin'.''

''He seduced her, right? Promised to marry her, but abandoned her at the last minute.''

''Well, I have no way of knowin' about the seducin' part, Jake,'' Augustus Bates responded, his tone suggesting he considered the subject indelicate in the extreme. ''And as for describin' his abandonment as last minute—well, the drownin' *did* occur more than a month before the weddin' date.''

''The . . . *what?*''

''The drownin'.''

''Harriman Gage drowned somebody?'' God, had the man been a murderer? That was one possibility Jake hadn't considered.

''Just himself.''

It took Jake a second to understand what this implied. ''Harriman Gage committed suicide to get out of marrying Caroline Anne?''

Beauregard whined suddenly.

''Hush, Beau,'' Augustus Bates said sharply. He seemed shocked. ''Suicide? Oh, my, no. It was quite accidental. He'd gone back to Boston, you see, to gather his belongin's and fully apprise his family of his plans. He went boatin' with some friends and—"

"Wait a minute," Jake interrupted. "Wait just a minute, Mr. Bates. Given the things I'd heard, I figured Gage was probably some two-timing married carpetbagger who got Caroline Anne pregnant and then ran off after kicking her dog and stealing the family silver! But you're telling me all this guy did was *drown?*"

"Well, he exercised decidedly poor judgment goin' out in a boat without knowin' how to swim," the older man returned stiffly. After a second his manner eased slightly and he continued more judiciously, "I suppose people hereabouts may go a bit overboard—pardon that tacky pun—in their condemnation of Harriman Gage. Still, there's no disputin' he blighted Caroline Anne Barnwell's life beyond repair."

Jake forked his fingers back through his hair. "But it wasn't his fault. It just happened."

"I don't believe anythin' just happens, Jake," Augustus Bates declared, bending over to stroke his dog. After a moment he straightened and continued speaking. "Oh, I'll admit circumstances can overwhelm every now and again. But the pure and simple fact is that people have to be held accountable for what they do." He paused a beat, cocking his head. "By the way, has anyone ever told you bear a small but definitely discernible resemblance to a pencil sketch of Harriman Gage?"

Seven

"Would y'all like another roll or biscuit?" the waitress inquired, thrusting a napkin-lined basket beneath Callie's nose.

Callie breathed in deeply, wrestling with temptation. The yeasty aroma emanating from the basket was heady enough to induce intoxication. Her mouth watered.

"Mmm...no, thank you," she said finally, giving the young server a regretful smile.

The waitress shifted the basket toward Jake. "Would y'all like another roll or biscuit?" she asked.

Jake shook his head. "None for me, thanks."

Looking vaguely disappointed, the young woman nodded and moved off to the next table.

Callie sighed contentedly, then smiled across the table at Jake. "I feel like one of Stella Avery's stage props."

Jake chuckled, understanding her sense of satiation. The dinner they'd just shared had been one of the best he'd ever had—though not just because of the food. "Stuffed, you mean?"

"Exactly."

They were sitting at a table for two on the glassed-in terrace of what was widely considered one of the best restaurants in the county. The ambiance wasn't particularly fancy, but the food was home-cooked heavenly. Callie had been quick to suggest it several days before when Jake had proposed that they have dinner together.

This dinner was not a date. It was simply a night out shared by two friends. Callie knew that. And she knew Jake knew it, too.

She was aware, of course, that some people might not understand the distinction. Her aunt and half brother, for example. But, since the two of them were off in Atlanta for the weekend, this likely failure of understanding didn't much matter. She had no intention of telling either one of them about her dinner with Jake.

Jake took a drink from the glass of wine at his elbow. "You know, I think I've become addicted to that roast I ordered," he commented, mentally savoring the memory of his entrée. "Who would've thought that beef basted with Coca-Cola would taste so good?"

"Anyone born and bred in the South," Callie informed him. "Coke is mother's milk down here."

"Oh, really? And here I thought the beverage of choice was moonshine."

"That's another state over."

"Ah."

Callie licked her lips. "The roast was good," she conceded. "But my personal downfall was that brandy-spiked chestnut soufflé."

Jake shifted slightly, wondering if she knew how provocative the movement of her pink tongue over her softly glossed mouth was. "You did pretty well by the fried okra, too," he teased, then found himself on the receiving end of a reproachful look.

"A true gentleman wouldn't point that out."

Jake lifted his brows, laughter glinting in his blue-green eyes. "I never claimed to be a gentleman, sweetheart. True or otherwise."

His casual use of the endearment triggered a sweet flutter of response within Callie. It was a sensation she'd become unsettlingly familiar with during the past week. She'd also become adept at ignoring it.

"Well, considerin' your clothes, I thought y'all might be *aspirin'* to be one," she returned, deliberately intensifying her drawl.

Callie had been unable to disguise her astonishment earlier in the evening when she'd come downstairs from her bedroom and gotten her first glimpse of a totally transformed Jake Turner. She'd known he planned to eschew his usual jeans and T-shirt—he'd told her as much when he'd suggested they go out to dinner. But she hadn't known those ordinary garments would be replaced by an impeccably cut suit, discreetly monogrammed white shirt and silk tie. Nor had she realized that Jake would wear his obviously designer duds the same way he wore his denims—with an offhand panache and innate masculine elegance.

Jake feigned modesty. "This old thing?" Although clothes were not a priority with him, he had a definite weakness for Italian tailoring. He justified his indulgence of this weakness by telling himself that not all his clients were comfortable with his usual blue-collar appearance.

Callie let her gaze drift over him. Even his usually tousled hair was neatly brushed. It gleamed like the tawny pelt of a healthy lion, tempting her to touch it. She recalled, just for an instant, what it had felt like to tangle her fingers in the crisp hair at the nape of Jake's neck when they'd kissed beneath one of the great trees at Quarter Oaks.

She cleared her brain of that memory and her throat of a sudden tightness. Then she commented casually, "Unless I've completely lost my eye, that 'old thing' is by Georgio Armani."

"Your eye's just fine, Callie. I'm impressed."

"Well, fashion *is* my business, Jake."

He tipped his head, acknowledging her point. "And, speaking of fashion—are you wearing one of your own designs tonight?"

Callie smiled, flattered that he'd noticed. "As a matter of fact, I am."

"It's very becoming." The swirly, sea-colored dress was distracting in the extreme, as well, in Jake's opinion. The bustier-style bodice of the garment hugged the upper part of Callie's body like a lover. The dress also nipped in at the waist, emphasizing her slenderness, then belled out into a floaty, petal-hemmed skirt. While the skirt didn't cling or catch, something about it made Jake very conscious of the curving feminine figure beneath.

Callie touched a hand to her hair. She felt pleased by his compliment. Maybe a bit too pleased, all things considered.

"Thank you," she said after a moment.

"You're welcome."

There was a small break in the conversation as the waitress returned to clear the table and take their dessert orders. Although the young woman urged them to try what she called a "coupe de goo"—a chocolate cake buried beneath fresh vanilla ice cream, fudge sauce, toasted pecans and whipped cream—they both opted for strawberry cobbler.

"Have you always been interested in clothes?" Jake asked after they'd been served their desserts.

Callie forked up a ruby-red berry and ate it. "Pretty much. I think I told you my father ran a dry-goods business out of the shop where Callie's Corner is now. He used to say that I started feeling fabrics when I was a baby. My mother taught me how to sew when I was little. The first things I made were dresses for my dolls. Eventually I graduated to making dresses for myself. By the time I was thirteen or fourteen, I knew I wanted a career in fashion. I nearly died from excitement when I got accepted at a design school in New York."

"Was it hard making the transition?"

"From a small Southern town to Manhattan, you mean?"

Jake nodded.

"I felt like a homesick hick in the beginning," Callie confessed with a self-deprecating smile. "I swear some of the students went out of their way to shock me. Not that they had to go very far in the beginning. I spent so much time with my mouth hanging open that one of my friends claimed she was able to memorize the exact location of all my fillings. Still, I learned to adjust. I toned down my accent as much as I could. I read everything form the *New York Times* to the *New York Post*. I even learned to stop eating Goo-Goo Clusters and start eating things like lox and bagels." She smiled again. "I guess that saying about the Lord protecting the innocent and the ignorant is true. There's no other explanation for my surviving as well as I did during my first few months in the Big Apple."

"Have you ever thought about going back?"

Callie's curving smile gave way to a small frown. She turned her head slightly, gazing out the terrace windows. It was dark and rainy outside. While late afternoon had arrived with a light drizzle, the evening had produced a full-scale summer thunderstorm. Mother Nature was putting on an electrifying display. The lights in the restaurant had flickered several times since they'd sat down.

"Yes, I've thought about it," she confessed slowly, almost sadly. "I loved New York. The excitement. The challenge. School was wonderful. And my first job was terrific. But I've got responsibilities in Deacon's Crossing. Aunt Henny. P.D. And my shop." She slanted a glance at Jake. "I know it's never going to be the springboard to my becoming the second Donna Karan, but I think Callie's Corner has turned out pretty well."

Now it was Jake's turn to avert his gaze. He studied the serving of cobbler in front of him, wondering if he had any right to ask the questions he wanted to ask. The Lord protects the innocent, Callie had said a few moments ago. Just how "innocent" had she been when she'd gone to New

York? How much of herself had she given to the fiancé Bernice the waitress had mentioned so unfavorably? Was it memories of that man which had shadowed her features with melancholy just a few moments before?

Jake lifted his eyes and looked across the table at Callie. She was nibbling on a forkful of cobbler. He tried not to focus on the delicate movements of her teeth and tongue, but it was impossible. The memory of the single, searing kiss they'd shared arrowed through him. The recollection of heat and hunger settled heavily between his thighs. He clenched one hand beneath the table.

"You're not my type," he'd told her. And she'd agreed. She'd accepted. He knew she had. So why was his body—if not his brain—refusing to do the same?

"You were engaged, weren't you?" he asked. The tone of the question was blunt, almost bludgeoning. Jake wished he could take it back and soften it. But since he couldn't, he decided to let it stand.

Callie's breath caught briefly at the top of her throat. She set down her fork, studying the man sitting opposite her for several seconds.

"P.D.?" she asked, guessing at the source of his information. She was uncertain how she felt about the fact that Jake clearly knew things about her she hadn't told him.

Jake had garnered a bit about her engagement from her half brother, but he couldn't pretend that's where he'd first learned of it.

"Bernice at Earle's All You Can Eat," he admitted.

"Small towns, no secrets," Callie summed up. Her mind flashed back to the lunch she and Jake had had at the café four days before. Had Bernice heard their exchange about affairs? she wondered uncomfortably. And, if she had, had she said anything to anybody?

"I wasn't prying, Callie," Jake said. This was true, up to a point. After all, Bernice had volunteered the first comment about his dinner companion's unlucky love life. Of course, he hadn't exactly let the matter drop. Still he wouldn't call what he'd done *prying*. The questions he'd asked the waitress had been more a matter of priming the pump.

"You weren't?"

"All right. Maybe. Yes. A little. But when Bernice mentioned you'd been engaged, I got…curious. These last two weeks you've never said anything about it." And the two weeks before that, as Jake well knew, she'd probably have preferred being deep-fried in peanut oil to revealing a shred of her personal background to him.

"I *was* engaged," Callie confirmed after a pause. "His name was Mark Stephens. He was—still is, I assume—a lawyer. We met at a gallery opening in SoHo about eight years ago."

"And you fell in love."

"Yes," Callie responded then hesitated, reconsidering. Strange. She'd spent years thinking of Mark Stephens as the man who'd broken her heart. Yet at this very moment she had trouble recalling what he looked or sounded like. "At least, I thought I did. We dated for about six months, then we moved in together."

"I see." Half of Jake wanted her to stop talking. The other half wanted her to tell him everything. So Callie had lived with this Mark Stephens. She'd slept with him. She'd wanted to be the man's wife!

"After about a year," Callie resumed, trying to keep her voice level, "we decided we would get married. We started making plans. Preparations. And then…one awful night…I got a call from Aunt Henny telling me my stepmother was dead and my father was in an intensive care unit."

There was pain in her voice. In her eyes. Jake couldn't stand to see her hurting simply to satisfy his need to know. He reached across the table and covered one of her hands with his own.

"Callie, you don't have to tell me this," he said.

She shook her head, the press of Jake's hard palm making her tremble just a little.

"No. I want to tell you," she said firmly. It was the truth, she realized. She really did want to tell him. Exactly why, she didn't know. But it was suddenly important for Jake to hear her story from her, not someone else.

"It's odd," she continued. "Everyone around Deacon's Crossing pretty much knows what happened between Mark and me. Or at least they think they do. But I've never told anyone the story. Not even Aunt Henny."

Jake said nothing. He simply waited for her to go on.

Callie sighed again, easing her hand out from under his. The contact was too distracting. "I flew back to Deacon's Crossing on the first plane I could get. Mark came with me. He seemed very supportive."

"But—?"

"The accident happened in late June. We were planning to get married in early September. But we decided to postpone the wedding. A few days after my stepmother's funeral, Mark went back to New York."

"And that was it?" Had the guy just bailed out? Jake wondered angrily. Was that what Bernice had meant when she'd said that Callie had been deserted by her fiancé in her time of tribulation?

Callie was caught off guard by the sudden flash of temper she saw in Jake's eyes. There were small white indentations at the corners of his mouth, as though he was struggling to keep from speaking. The muscles in his neck were visibly knotted.

"Oh—no, no," she said hurriedly, shaking her head. "We talked on the telephone. Daily at first. Then...less frequently. He expected me to get things settled and come back to New York, you see. But I couldn't. I knew I was going to have to stay in Deacon's Crossing. Somebody had to look after my father, my aunt and my brother, and I was the only person available. I tried to explain the situation to Mark. During our last conversation I even raised the idea of his moving to Deacon's Crossing. He lost his temper and told me that he'd spent years getting out of some tiny town in Idaho, and he had no intention of ending up in the boondocks of Georgia. I...well, I lost my temper, too. I asked him where that left us, and he said that as far as he was concerned, there wasn't any 'us' anymore. He said he'd thought we were two of a kind. Then he said that if I was the type who could be happy staying in Deacon's Crossing, that obviously wasn't so.''

Callie's use of the word *type* sliced into Jake like a knife. "Bastard," he muttered.

Callie smiled crookedly. "No. Mark was just being honest."

There was a short, sharp silence. Jake found himself breathing a prayer of gratitude that Callie hadn't added ''like you'' to her last sentence.

"You . . . never thought about moving everybody back to New York with you?" he asked finally. "Of taking care of them there?"

Callie lowered her lashes for a few seconds. "Yes, I thought about it," she admitted, not proud of the selfishness this implied. "But I realized I couldn't. You see, Deacon's Crossing is my family's home." She raised her eyes and looked squarely at Jake. "It's *my* home."

Callie's home was dark when she pulled up in front of it about ninety minutes later. She and Jake had taken her car to the restaurant rather than his pickup. Unlike some men, he'd had no problem with being chauffeured by a woman.

A flash of lightning ripped the ink-black sky.

A moment later there was a powerful rumble of thunder.

"Didn't we leave some lights on when we left?" Jake asked as Callie set the brake and turned off the engine. A small portion of his brain noted his use of the plural pronoun and wondered about it. *We?* Since when had he started talking in terms of *we?*

"I'm pretty sure we did," Callie answered, surveying the front of the house. She glanced to her right, just barely able to discern the expression on Jake's face. "I've got a bad feeling about this."

"Yeah," he concurred, nodding his head. He remembered the way the lights had flickered in the restaurant. "I'll bet the storm's knocked down a power line someplace."

"You know, now that I think about it, I didn't see any lights on at either of the other houses on this road."

Jake undid his seat belt and leaned forward to retrieve the umbrella at his feet. "Look, you take this and head for the porch," he said. "I'm going to make a run to my truck. I've got a flashlight in the glove compartment."

"You'll get drenched!" Callie protested.

"I'm tough. I can take it," he returned with a wry chuckle, then started to shrug out of his jacket. Although he was washable, the custom-tailored garment definitely wasn't.

"Are you sure?" She took the keys out of the ignition. The rain was beating a tattoo on the roof of the car.

"Positive. Now go."

Despite the umbrella, Callie was in a pretty bedraggled state by the time she reached the porch. Her hair was wildly windblown, her dress damp, and her stocking-clad legs spattered with Georgia mud. The stylish high-heeled sandals she had on were ruined. They made squishy little sounds as she crossed to the front door.

"Ugh," she said with a shiver, brushing her tangled hair back from her face. She began fumbling with her keys, trying to figure out which one fit the front door. Given the darkness, she had only her sense of touch to rely on.

She was still fumbling when Jake dashed up onto the porch.

"Here," he said, shining the flashlight he'd retrieved on her hands. Although he'd run the entire distance from the car to the truck to the porch, his breathing pattern was unruffled.

Callie glanced at him, then made a sound of dismay. "You're soaked, Jake!"

"Tell me about it," he returned, flashing a rueful grin. He raked his fingers through his sodden hair, grimacing at the rivulets of water he felt running down his face and neck. He wiped his cheeks with his palms. The fabric of his shirt was sticking to his chest like wet tissue paper. It was not one of the more pleasant sensations he'd ever experienced.

A few moments later, Callie inserted the correct key into the front door lock and opened it. A moment after that, they were both inside the house.

"God!" Jake exclaimed feelingly, shutting the door.

Callie seconded this sentiment as she kicked off her sandals. She then felt for the foyer light switch.

"At least we can say we know enough to come in out of the rain," she joked, locating the switch. She clicked it on and off. Nothing happened.

"True. But we'll also have to admit we're still in the dark," Jake returned, picking up her quip. He, too, kicked off his shoes. They thudded against the hall's wooden floor. "Do you have any candles? Or maybe a kerosene lamp?"

Callie nodded. "Candles in the—" A sneeze tickled her nose. "Ah-choo! Candles in the kitchen. And a lamp, I think."

"Great. Let's—" Jake broke off abruptly, his ears registering an odd noise.

"Jake?" Callie asked, the skin on the nape of her neck suddenly prickling.

"Did you hear that?"

"Hear what?"

Jake cocked his head, listening. Yeah. There it was again. A high-pitched whimpering. Not very distinct, but definitely there.

"Jake?" Callie whispered uncertainly, pressing a hand against his arm.

The warmth of her palm and fingers penetrated the clammy fabric of Jake's shirt, heating the rain-cooled skin beneath. Lower down in his body, masculine muscles suddenly clenched.

"I think it's coming from upstairs," Jake said in a voice that missed its normal tone by a note or two. "You stay here. I'll go check it out."

"But—"

"I'll be right back, Callie," he promised, disengaging from her touch. He took an instant to stroke a teasing finger across the curve of her lower lip, then headed up to the second floor.

Jake was out of Callie's sight for no more than ninety seconds. The flashlight he was carrying threw weirdly shaped shadows on the walls when he reappeared at the top of the staircase. It also revealed that he was wearing a rather bemused expression.

"Jake?" Callie asked, taking a step forward.

"I think I may need some help up here," he announced calmly, palming his hair back from his brow.

"What's happened?"

"What's happened?" he echoed. "What's happened is that Buttercup's decided to become a mother all over my bed."

Eight

Oh, no, Callie thought, staring at Jake Turner as though she was seeing him for the first time. In a way, she was. No.

"Easy, girl, easy," Jake murmured.

This wasn't supposed to happen, she told herself. She was like some cartoon character who'd just discovered she'd stepped off a cliff into thin air. She knew she was doomed, but she hadn't yet started to plummet downward. But at any moment now. Any moment...

"That'sa girl," Jake continued in the same soothing voice.

Callie knitted her fingers together to hide their trembling. The fabric of her emotional certainty was unraveling. The foundation of her life was breaking into millions of tiny pieces.

"Good dog," Jake said softly, petting Henrietta Barnwell's much-loved mongrel with a slow, rhythmic stroke. "Good Buttercup. Yes. Yes. Good Buttercup."

Nearly an hour had passed since Jake's announcement from the top of the stairs. Callie had rushed up to the second floor and into his bedroom only to discover that Buttercup had already done all the real work connected with giving birth to five healthy puppies. The only tasks left for Callie and Jake involved offering congratulations and cleaning up.

It should have been easy. Unfortunately Buttercup had turned out to have some very definite ideas about her post-delivery treatment. With bared teeth and ominous growls, she'd made it clear that she didn't want Callie anywhere near her or her new babies. Jake, however, had been allowed to get as close and cozy as he chose.

Buttercup had snuffled approvingly as he'd examined each one of her puppies. She'd also submitted to his examination of her, then nosed his palm, encouraging him to pet her. And once he'd started petting, she hadn't wanted him to stop.

At first Callie had found the dog's demand for Jake's attention both amusing and endearing. But then, gradually, her response to what she was seeing changed. She'd become mesmerized by the almost tangible bond between man and animal. Her eyes had been irresistibly, inevitably, drawn to the slow, steady movements of Jake's hands over the obviously trusting Buttercup.

Jake's hands.

Such strong, sure hands. The hands of a man accustomed to performing manual labor. Sinewy hands. Sensual hands. The hands of an artist as well as an artisan.

Competent hands.

Careful hands.

Kind hands, too.

This last realization had sidled into Callie's brain unbidden, setting off unexpected reverberations deep within her. It had deflected her train of thought from hands to the whole man.

Jake Turner...kind?

He'd scoffed when she'd called him nice, and perhaps he'd been right. *Nice* was too weak a word for so strong a man. But...*kind?*

Yes. Kind. How else to describe a man who'd take time to comfort a whining dog, counsel a wayward teenager and cosset a little old lady? He'd deny it to himself and the world until his dying day, no doubt. And, given the emotional kicks and bruises she knew he'd suffered, Callie thought she understood why. But his denials didn't change the fact that he was kind. Kinder in his fashion, in fact, than almost anyone she'd ever met.

But kind was not all he was.

Callie had never encountered a man like Jake Turner. She'd never really dreamed anyone like him existed. He'd shaken her to the core the moment they'd met, and he'd gone on disrupting her life ever since.

He was provocative.

Passionate.

A pain in the neck.

He was attractive.

Intelligent.

And infuriating in the extreme.

She had absolutely nothing in common with him. Nothing! And yet there were moments when she felt such a sense of connection with him....

"You and I are two entirely different kinds of people, Callie," he'd told her at Quarter Oaks. *"You're hello. I'm goodbye. You're rooted in this town. I've got a two-month lease. There's no way things could work out between us."*

He'd repeated this theme at irregular intervals ever since the first and only kiss they'd shared. He'd repeated it as though there was a danger that one of them might forget the fundamental truth of their relationship if he didn't.

"I don't celebrate Christmas, Easter, Thanksgiving or Mother's Day," he'd informed her once, his tone declarative, not defiant. *"I've got a post office box for a permanent address, and I spend a lot of time living out of the back of a pickup truck. That's how I want it, Callie. I have no intention of getting married and I don't give a damn about carrying on the Turner name. I work in wood. If I leave any*

legacy when I go, it'll be the things I've made with my hands."

Jake Turner was rootless in every real sense of the word. He was adamantly uncommitted to places or people. He was the last man in the world she'd ever expected to like, much less to fall in love with. And yet...

And yet, sweet heaven, that was exactly what she'd done.

"This wasn't supposed to happen," Callie whispered. But she knew it had. Somehow, some way, she'd lost her heart to a man who didn't want it, who would refuse to take it even if he did.

Jake looked up. "What did you say?" he asked quietly, the promise of a smile tugging at the corners of his lips.

Because Buttercup's preferences had made her presence in this room virtually superfluous, Callie had gone down to the kitchen several times to fetch supplies. Among the items she'd brought upstairs was a kerosene lamp. It now burned on a small table to the right of the bed, illuminating the room.

The glow from the lamp seemed to emphasize the virility of Jake's features. It underscored the angled strength of his cheekbones and the potent sensuality of his mobile mouth. It gilded the surface of his deeply tanned skin and the tawny strands of his tousled hair.

Callie stared at him, praying that the storm of feelings inside her didn't show on her face.

"Callie?" Jake's tone sharpened. A faint line appeared between his brows. The hint of the smile she'd seen only a moment before vanished.

"I'm going downstairs to get a few more things," she answered, astonished that she could summon up the words and speak them clearly. "Some more towels... and some candles. I'll be back in a few minutes."

Callie had the feeling he was on the verge of saying something, then thought better of it.

"I'll be here," he promised.

* * *

Jake was never certain how long Callie was gone, but he knew it was longer than a few minutes. Indeed, it felt like hours before he heard the soft sounds that heralded her return to the second floor.

Callie's lengthy absence had been both a boon and a bane. A boon because it gave him the time to lull Buttercup to sleep then to head off to the bathroom for a much-needed washing up. A bane because it also afforded him an unbroken interval in which to contemplate all the possible meanings of the extraordinary expression he'd glimpsed in Callie's eyes before she'd gone downstairs.

His contemplations had renewed, then redoubled, the heated heaviness that had throbbed below his belt earlier in the evening. This had reminded him—as if he needed reminding!—of how much he'd come to want Callie Barnwell.

Jake came out of the bathroom as soon as his ears registered her light footfall. He met Callie in the hallway, just a few paces from the top of the stairs. He was still drying his hands. She was carrying a lighted candle in a hammered silver holder.

"Problems?" he questioned, watching her intently. The flickering of the candle flame lent a mysterious quality to her hazel eyes. Her lids looked heavier and her sable-colored lashes lusher than he remembered.

Callie shook her head. "No," she answered softly. "Why?"

The candlelight licked the skin of her slender throat and softly rounded shoulders. Jake felt a sharp, sudden urge to do the same. He waged and won a battle to control the urge, but he couldn't make it go away.

"You were gone a long time," he said. She was close enough so he could smell the elusive floral scent of her perfume.

Callie lifted her chin. Most of her hair fell away from her face but a few strands clung stubbornly to her right cheek. "Did you miss me, Jake?" she asked.

Maybe it was the way she spoke his name. Maybe it was simply the temptation of her softly rounded cheek. But something overruled Jake's common sense and made him reach out and brush the errant strands of hair off Callie's face. He hooked them behind her ears, letting his fingertips linger on her skin for a moment longer than necessary. When he withdrew his hand, it was less than steady.

"Yes, I missed you," he replied bluntly. "What were you doing down there?"

She hesitated, then answered softly, "Thinking."

"About what?"

Another hesitation. An even softer answer. "You."

The single-word admission hit him like a sledgehammer. "What about . . . me?" he asked after several pulsating seconds.

Callie glanced sideways for a moment. Jake heard her catch her breath, saw her breasts rise against the tightly fitted bodice of her dress. He had the impression she was gathering her resolve. This impression solidified into certainty when she shifted her eyes back to his.

"I was thinking about your hands, Jake," she said huskily. "I was thinking about what it would be like to have them touching me."

Jake had spent most of his thirty-five years deliberately building barricades against the world. While he'd let down a few of them—some willingly, others not so—since he'd come to Deacon's Crossing, his defenses were still very, very strong. Even so, he found himself rocked to the center of his heavily armored soul by the devastating honesty of Callie's reply.

"Callie—" he began, dropping the towel he'd been holding.

"I was thinking about my hands, too," she went on. "And I was thinking about what it would be like to have them touching you."

"Callie—" Jake tried again. His voice was taut. So was his body.

"Have you ever thought about either of those things, Jake?"

Had he ever thought—

"Yes," he admitted harshly. "Yes, I've thought about my hands and your hands. And yes, I've thought about me touching you and you touching me. But it won't work, Callie."

She moved closer to him. The expression he thought he'd seen earlier was back in her eyes, overlaid with something that might have been determination or desperation or a strange mixture of both.

"Why not?" she asked, lifting her free hand and placing it very gently against his chest.

"You know why not." Jake caught her hand with one of his own, intending to pull it away. He ended up pressing it closer. The warmth of her soft palm and slender fingers branded him to the bone. "We've talked about the reasons."

"Maybe I don't think those reasons are valid anymore. Maybe I've decided that our being totally different doesn't mean we can't be together for now. For tonight."

Jake shook his head vehemently, denying the possibility. "You're not a one-night stand, Callie."

She flexed her fingers as though testing the muscled resilience of his chest. "Two nights, then," she countered. "This is Friday. We have the house to ourselves until Sunday."

Desire clawed at Jake, raking him with a bittersweet urgency that was part agony, part promised ecstasy. It required more discipline than he'd realized he had not to take anything and everything Callie seemed to be offering right then and there.

"I'm leaving at the end of the month," he reminded her. "I'm leaving and I'm not coming back."

"I know, Jake," she responded with the same soul-shaking candor she'd used before. "I know and I don't care. I want this. You and me. Us. Tonight. And tomorrow night. And for as many nights as you want until you go."

Jake caught her chin between thumb and forefinger and tilted it up. He searched her face, feature by feature. She met his gaze steadily, her eyes warm, her mouth welcoming. He saw no signs of tricks or traps.

"Callie," he began almost prayerfully. "Dear God, Callie. Are you sure?"

The smile she gave him reduced his control to a fraying thread. Her next words nearly snapped it.

"Yes, I'm sure," she answered. "I'm even…prepared."

Jake exhaled in a sudden rush. "Prepared—?"

Callie went up on tiptoe. He felt the lick of her tongue before he heard her whisper, "I never gave back what I found in P.D.'s jeans."

Against the darkness of Callie's bedroom, one candle burned while two people were willingly consumed by an incandescent flame.

"Kiss me," Jake whispered thickly. He wanted to taste her mouth again. To feel her sweet lips tremble then open to him. To have her tongue slide over his. "Kiss me, Callie."

She did, giving him all he wanted and more. Her lips were parting even as he lowered his head. There was no need for him to coax or cajole. Callie met his need and matched it. The movements of her moist, pliant mouth communicated both yielding and yearning. The broken little sounds she made when his tongue began to claim the softness behind her lips was an arousing mix of plea and pleasure.

They were both shaking when the kiss came to an end.

"Yes," Callie murmured, gazing up at Jake with hunger-hazed eyes. "Oh, yes."

She began to undo the small buttons on the front of his shirt. The unsteadiness of her fingers complicated what should have been an easy task. Finally, though, she completed the job. She tugged the garment free of his trousers and eased it off his shoulders. At the same moment that she began to pull the sleeves down his arms, she stepped in close, brushing her mouth against the tautly muscled torso she'd just exposed. She inhaled deeply, savoring the clean masculine scent of his skin.

She murmured his name, her warm breath stirring the coarse silk hair on his chest. She lapped at him with her tongue and gloried in his shuddering response.

"Callie, sweetheart," he said hoarsely. "Do you have any idea what you're doing to me?"

One discreetly monogrammed white shirt fluttered to the floor, unwanted and unnecessary.

Jake circled Callie's waist, drawing her tight against him, letting her feel the hard proof of his need. She moved her hips once, turning the ache in his groin into something close to agony. He growled deep in his throat.

He tracked up the path of the zipper set into the back of her dress until he found the tab at the top. He began to pull it downward very slowly. Millimeter...by millimeter...the garment closing gave way. The tightly fitted bodice parted.

Callie quivered when she felt the stroke of Jake's fingertips against the naked skin of her back. He drew a teasing line along her spine, sending wild, white-hot shivers cascading through her body. She clung to him, quivering.

Jake bared Callie's breasts, then covered them with his hands. Her softly mounded flesh blossomed against the hard, hungry curves of his palms. He teased her nipples with the pads of his thumbs until they stiffened into tight, twin buds. Angling his head, he kissed the side of her neck. He teased her with his tongue and teeth. Nuzzling. Nibbling. Nipping. He left no marks, but the claim he staked on her smooth, creamy skin was unmistakable.

Callie's head tilted back, her throat arching. Her eyes fluttered closed for an instant. She kneaded Jake's chest with her fingers, seeking out the taut buttons of his male nipples. When she found the small, rigid nubbins of flesh, she raked them delicately with her nails.

Jake groaned.

A second or two later, Callie's swirly, sea-colored dress lay puddled around her slim ankles.

More kisses. Caresses.

"All of you," Jake said, his voice hot and husky. "I need to see all of you. To have all of you."

Callie felt the same way.

They shed the rest of their clothes with impatient hands. Naked, he embraced her.

Naked, she embraced him.

"I want you so much, Callie."

"I want you even more, Jake."

They moved to the bed. Succumbing to the firm but gentle urging of Jake's hands, Callie sank down on the edge of the mattress. Boldly she let her eyes travel up his body. She had assessed him as all male, all muscle, within the first few minutes they'd met. She realized now that this assessment had been an understatement of his potency.

"Don't look at me like that, sweetheart." Jake's voice was deep and just a little dangerous.

Callie's smile was like a caress. "Why not?"

"Because I'll lose what little control I have if you do."

The idea made her shiver with a mixture of pleasurable anticipation and primitively feminine apprehension. "What's wrong with that?"

Jake showed his teeth. "I'm not . . . prepared."

It took Callie a moment to understand. "Oh."

"Where—?"

Flushing, she nodded toward the small stand at the head of her bed. "Top drawer," she answered.

"Help me," Jake suggested provocatively a few moments later.

After a split second of hesitation, Callie complied. It was something she'd never done before. The fleeting awkwardness she felt quickly dissolved in the erotic intimacy of the act. She learned, beyond any question, that women who thought precautions and passion didn't mix were totally mistaken.

And then Jake joined her on the bed. They stretched out together. Touching. Tantalizing. Testing.

Jake kissed a burning path down to Callie's right breast.
He licked the pouting tip once, twice, then began to suckle
on it with tender ferocity. Her already ragged breathing
pattern tore in two as she cried out in answer to the sensations he was evoking. She brought her hands up, tunneling
her fingers into the hair on the back of his head, holding
him against her.

After many, many moments, Jake transferred his attentions to her left breast. By this time she was caressing his
shoulders and back, the ever-changing stroke and pressure
of her hands communicating both demand and desire.

"Oh, Jake...yes. Jake!" she whispered, savoring the feel
of his rippling muscles. A wave of possessiveness washed
through her. She scored his skin lightly with her nails, relishing the way he shuddered and gasped her name.

And then it was Callie's turn to shudder and gasp as Jake
slid one of his hands down the length of her body and
slipped it between her legs. She shifted and opened to him.
His fingers stroked through the silken cluster of curls at the
apex of her thighs. He teased her for several sweet and
searing moments, then sought more intimate access to her
womanly secrets.

A small kernel of flesh throbbed within the protective
folds of Callie's petaled femininity. Jake found it, finessed
it. He brushed his fingers against it with infinite care. When
Callie opened her mouth to cry out her response, he bent his
head and claimed both her mouth and the cry for his own.

"J-Jake," she breathed when he finally lifted his lips. She
gazed up into his face. Despite the dim illumination in the
room, she could see the strain in his features. His tanned
skin was pulled taut over strong, angled bones. His eyes had
gone very dark.

She lifted a trembling hand and brushed it against the
strong line of his jaw. He turned his head slightly, his breath
fanning her knuckles. He was still stroking her intimately,
gauging her passion, giving her pleasure.

"Please..."

Jake eased Callie slowly onto her back. Then, just as slowly, he shifted his body to cover hers. He was nearly undone by the sudden feel of her slender fingers closing around the blunt length of his arousal.

"Cal-lie!" A jolt of sensation that was half pleasure, half pain made him fracture her name.

"Now," she urged. *"Now."*

He couldn't have held back if he'd wanted to. And he didn't want to. He joined them in one smooth thrust, burying himself within her liquid heat. The momentum of that initial merging almost sent him tumbling over the edge, but he caught himself. Too soon, he told himself. Too soon.

Sheathed and double sheathed, Jake held himself very still. He smoothed Callie's hair back from her forehead. Her brow sheened with perspiration. Her skin was feverish to the touch.

"Oh, sweetheart . . ." he whispered.

Stunned by the passionate fullness of Jake's possession, Callie lay still as well. What little breath she had leaked out of her lungs on a melting sigh. She'd never known. She'd never imagined . . .

Languidly, she rocked her pelvis. She heard Jake groan. Saw his lips draw back from his teeth.

"Now," she whispered for the third time.

Jake began to move. Slowly at first, then faster and faster. Callie raised her hips, meeting his thrusts. Something inside her tightened, then tightened again.

"Oh. . . ."

"Yes."

"I can't . . ."

"You can."

Jake felt the first convulsive fluttering of Callie's release. He thrust one final time, overcome by the urgency of his own appetites. She shuddered. So did he. Mutual passion sundered all considerations but the shared need for satisfaction.

"Jake!"

"Callie!"

A month's worth of sparks ignited an explosion of ecstasy that lasted for an unknowable amount of time.

During that time, two very different types of people became one.

"Callie?"

"Mmm?"

"Are you . . . all right?"

Callie would have laughed if she hadn't understood the uncertainty that lay behind his question. Like her, Jake was beginning to recover from the earth-shattering consummation they'd just experienced. But unlike her, his return to normal was accompanied by the renewal of doubts.

She'd confronted and conquered her doubts an eternity ago—in the kitchen, while supposedly gathering towels and candles. No matter what happened from this night on, those doubts would not come back to haunt her.

"Never better," she said throatily. Turning her head a little, she pressed a kiss against his corded neck, tasting the salty tang of dried perspiration. Jake stirred. His hair-roughened leg rubbed against her smooth ones.

"I never intended for this to happen, Callie," he told her after several moments.

Callie shifted so she could look at him. "I did," she answered simply, steadily. The two words were the absolute and unadulterated truth.

His nostrils flared on a wild intake of breath. "Callie—"

She silenced him by brushing her mouth over his. "No," she whispered fiercely. She kissed one corner of his lips and then the other. "Don't say it."

Jake made a sound that was half groan of pleasure, half growl of protest. "Callie, I don't want to hurt you," he told her huskily, his vivid eyes glinting beneath heavy lids.

"You haven't," she assured him, her voice quiet but convincing in its intensity. "You won't. Don't you understand? You've been honest with me. Now let me be honest with you. I know exactly what we can have together. I know exactly how long we can have it. And I want it, Jake. I want it all.''

Jake stared at Callie for several sizzling seconds, his eyes growing darker and darker. Then, suddenly, his arms came around her. He pulled her soft body against his hard one. The crisp hair on his chest abraded her nipples. The rising strength of his manhood throbbed against her feminine cleft.

"So do I, sweetheart," he confessed rawly, stroking one hand up her spine. He cradled the back of her head, angling her face to receive his kiss. "So...do...I."

Callie awoke shortly after dawn. She was nestled in the possessive circle of Jake's strong arms, her cheek pressed against his broad chest. One of his knees rode intimately between her thighs.

She lay where she was, listening to the steady beat of her lover's heart. Calmly, quietly, she reviewed the daisy chain of discoveries and decisions that had brought her to this moment with this man.

She loved Jake Turner.
But she'd never tell him.
She loved Jake Turner.
Though he didn't love her in return.
She loved Jake Turner.
And if one brief month was all she could ever have with him, so be it.

"Better one month than none," Callie whispered to herself. "Better remembrances of what was...than regrets about what might have been but never happened."

Nine

Callie and Jake were together nearly every minute of the Saturday that followed the birth of Buttercup's puppies. It was a day of loving and laughter, of teasing and coming to terms. Nothing could mar it. Not even the realization that having Jake lounging around Callie's Corner like a pasha in a harem for eight hours straight was bound to be irresistible grist for the local gossip mill.

The fact that electricity wasn't restored to the Barnwell house until mid-evening didn't spoil anything, either—except the contents of the refrigerator. Yes, the combination of triple-digit August temperatures and no air conditioning was uncomfortable after their return from Callie's shop. But it was remarkable how refreshing a leisurely two-in-the-tub bath turned out to be.

It was also remarkable how many erotic uses Jake found for a sponge during the course of that rather protracted bath. To say nothing of what he did with a washcloth. And a piece of perfumed soap. He also got pretty creative when it came to the task of mopping up the many gallons of water they'd slopped out of the tub after his foreplay with props had erupted into a full-scale act of passion.

And then there were his suggestions about what they *could* have done in the tub—or, possibly, out of it—if they'd had a rubber duckie. Callie didn't know whether she should react to these suggestions by keeling over in shock or by calling around to local stores to find out if any of them had the squeaky yellow bath toy in stock. She settled for showing her new lover that he wasn't the only one with an outrageous imagination.

After their extended stay in the bathroom, Jake took Callie to bed. Although the power had come back on by that time, they made love by candlelight once again. The sheets were cool and crisp when they began; heated and damp when sleep finally claimed them.

They made love three more times before their idyllic weekend came to a close. The ecstasy Callie experienced during their third encounter was still echoing in her brain and blood when she greeted her returning relatives.

Henrietta and P.D. Barnwell came home bearing souvenirs and stories. But they were distracted from their desire to detail their adventures in Atlanta less than five minutes after their arrival. An announcement from Jake dramatically reordered their priorities.

"Oh, my," Callie's aunt gasped.

"Will you look at that," P.D. said admiringly.

"Oh my, oh my," Henrietta Barnwell repeated, holding a plump hand to her even plumper breast. "I *never* would have gone to Atlanta if I'd thought this was goin' to happen!"

"It's all right, Aunt Henny," Callie comforted, patting the older woman's shoulder. "There wouldn't have been much for you to do if you'd been here."

"I swear, she must really like you, Jake," P.D. said.

"Pretty remarkable, huh, kid?" Jake returned, grinning.

"I just feel so responsible, Callie," Aunt Henny continued. "After all, Buttercup *is* my dog."

"I wish I'd been here. I would've liked to see it happen, you know? I mean, I once watched this hamster of Seth Avery's have babies, but I was only a kid," P.D. informed Jake. "I don't remember much about it 'cept that his sister, Stella, walked in and started squealin' like a stuck pig."

"And that she went and had her babies on Jacob's bed, of all places! I am positively mortified beyond sayin' about that."

"No harm done, Aunt Henny," Callie declared reassuringly. She and her aunt were standing at the foot of Jake's bed. Jake was sitting on the edge of the mattress with Buttercup's head resting on his denimed thigh. P.D. was positioned on the opposite side of the bed.

"Will y'all just look at those puppies? Five of 'em. Five! Figure it'd be okay if I petted one, Jake?"

"Just take it slow and easy," Jake advised. "Buttercup's still pretty protective. She wouldn't even let Callie near the bed until this morning."

The excited expression on P.D.'s face made him seem more like six than sixteen. Callie watched him lean over and very carefully pat the head of the runt of the litter. Buttercup opened an eye and made a whuffling sound, but didn't shift her position.

"Hey," P.D. crooned to the puppy he was stroking. "Hey, little baby. Does this feel good to you?"

Jake chuckled. "Looks like you've got the magic touch, P.D."

Henny toddled around the bed to her nephew. "I s'pose it's too soon to tell what breeds they might be," she mused aloud.

Callie suppressed a laugh. "Aunt Henny, you've had Buttercup for years, and you still haven't figured out what breeds *she* is." After a moment's hesitation, she moved around to stand next to Jake. She felt an enjoyable illicit thrill when he glanced up and gave her a quick wink.

"I think there's a definite strain of basset hound in this litter, Miss Henny," he remarked casually, scratching between Buttercup's floppy ears.

"Basset hound?" P.D. echoed thoughtfully, transferring his attention to a second puppy.

"Basset hound?" Henrietta Barnwell pronounced the words as though they were synonymous with rabid wolf.

Callie frowned slightly. She'd never had any indication that her aunt harbored a prejudice against basset hounds. In fact, she'd never had any indication that her aunt harbored a prejudice against anything or anyone except—

"Augustus Bates has a basset hound," Jake observed.

Oh, no, Callie thought, suddenly understanding her aunt's attitude.

"That's right, he does," P.D. chimed in. "Named Beauregard. He told me a little 'bout him yesterday when we were at the Braves baseball game."

"Palmer Dean Barnwell the Third, are you sayin' you actually talked to that man while I was off shoppin' with Petal Conroy?" Henny demanded.

The teenager looked faintly abashed. "Well, to tell the honest truth, Aunt Henny...I, uh, kind of sat next to him."

"Did Mr. Bates bother you this weekend, Aunt Henny?" Callie asked, recalling the pledge of noninterference the newspaperman had made at Earle's All You Can Eat. "Because just last week he—"

The older woman was visibly horrified. "You've been talkin' to that man, too, Caroline Anne?"

"I guess I go in the—ah—doghouse as well, Miss Henny," Jake interpolated mildly. "Because I took Mr. Bates on a tour of Quarter Oaks the other day."

"P.D.—" Callie shot her half brother a questioning look.

"Mr. Bates was real nice," P.D. declared, answering her unvoiced concerns. He grimaced when his aunt made a choking sound of protest, but stuck to his guns when he turned his head toward the older woman and said, "Well, he was, Aunt Henny! And he didn't come within ten feet of you this whole weekend. Not once. I think maybe you're riled up because he didn't do anythin' rude. I think maybe you were hopin'—''

"P.D.,'' Jake said, cutting the teenager off. Callie noticed her half brother made no attempt to override the implied command to keep quiet.

"Didn't do anything rude?'' Henny repeated indignantly. "You don't think allowin' his dog to rampage loose and assault my poor Buttercup is rude?''

There was a brief silence. Callie and Jake traded looks. She found herself wishing that more than their eyes could touch. A sudden tightening in Jake's features suggested his desires might be running in the same direction. After gently easing Buttercup's head off his thigh, he rose from the bed. His body brushed against Callie's for one electric instant.

"Miss Henny, are you saying that Beauregard—ahem—imposed his attentions on Buttercup?'' he asked.

The older woman sniffed.

"Because if you are, I really think Mr. Bates should be called to account.''

Henny's eyes widened. "No!'' she said sharply, then softened the negative with a fluttery gesture. "No, thank you, Jacob. I don't believe that will be necessary. It—it was uncharitable of me to cast aspersions on a poor dumb animal just because its owner is a...a...well, whatever. Don't pay any mind to what I said.''

"Are you sure, Miss Henny?'' Jake draped an arm over Callie's shoulders. He shifted his weight slightly, his hip bumping hers.

Callie caught her breath and struggled to control her expression. Before her aunt and half brother had come back, she and Jake had agreed that they would have to be very careful about their affair around the house. If this was his idea of being very careful, they were definitely due for a private talk.

Fortunately neither her aunt nor her half brother seemed to attach any significance to the way Jake was touching her.

"Positive, Jacob,'' Henny returned. She patted her silver hair for several seconds, then fanned one hand back and forth in front of her face. "I declare, it's become down-right close up in here, hasn't it? You'd think the air conditionin'd been turned off."

Callie felt Jake's fingers tighten. She wanted to look at him, but she didn't dare. She cleared her throat.

"Why don't we leave Buttercup and the puppies and go have some iced tea, Aunt Henny?" she suggested brightly. "Jake and I would really like to hear more about your weekend in Atlanta."

"Why, what a lovely idea," Henny responded with a charming smile. "And, of course, y'all have to tell me about your weekend, too. Jacob, dear, I hope you didn't find it too uncomfortable bein' turned out of your bed by my dog. Wherever did you end up sleepin' the last two nights?"

The month that followed seemed as sweet as summer peaches to Callie, and she allowed herself to feast her fill. Deep in her heart she knew she was going to have to pay dearly for her greed. She also knew she'd accepted the price in advance.

She'd love . . . discreetly.

He'd leave . . . undoubtedly.

And then, very simply, very steadily, she'd go on with her life.

"I think I've changed my mind, Jake."

"Oh, come on, Callie."

"I'm not sure I ought to do this."

"Try it, sweetheart. You'll like it."

"But—it's dangerous!"

"Not if you're with someone who knows what he's doing. And I definitely know what I'm doing. I've got years of experience under my belt."

That's not all you've got under your belt, Callie thought with a voluptuous shiver. She recalled, very vividly, a brief but gratifying interlude in the storeroom of Callie's Corner just the evening before.

"Callie?" Jake's voice was silken.

Callie flushed. "What if we tip over? You said that happens sometimes, Jake."

"We'll take it slow and easy. I promise."

"Well . . ."

"You know you want to do it, sweetheart. Come on. Grab hold of my shoulder."

After a moment's hesitation, Callie followed his instruction. She flexed her fingers against his taut flesh when she took hold of him. The warmth of his skin was evident through the stretchy fabric of his T-shirt. So was the ripple and release of his muscles in response to her touch.

"Okay," Jake encouraged, his voice a little husky. "Now, right leg up and over."

"Like—like this?" It seemed to Callie that she was beginning to sound a bit breathless.

"Yeah. Mmm—oh, yeah. Like that. Exactly like that. You're a natural."

Callie laughed, acutely aware of a sudden thrumming in her body. The sensation was very . . . stimulating. It spoke of power. Carefully controlled power, to be sure, but power nonetheless.

She breathed in deeply, inhaling Jake's scent. It was very clean, with just a hint of male musk. She shifted forward an inch or two, seeking the most comfortable position.

"For God's sake, don't squirm like that!" Jake said twisting abruptly. He reached behind him, slipping his arm around Callie's waist. A quiver of excitement danced up and down her spine when she felt his fingers splay in the small of her back. She gasped as she felt those same fingers slide downward to her denim-covered bottom. A moment later she was more or less plastered against Jake.

She had to squirm. Just a little.

"Now what do I do?" she asked eventually, wondering if Jake could feel the pounding of her heart the way she could feel his. Her breasts were pressed firmly against his back. She knew her nipples were taut.

"Squeeze me with your thighs."

"S-squeeze you," she repeated shakily. A sweet explosion of pleasure detonated deep inside her. Oh. Oh...God.

"Good, Callie. Now, put your arms around me and hold on—*no!* Not like—Callie! Are you trying to drive me crazy? Hold on a little higher!"

Callie moved her hands. "There?"

She heard—and felt—Jake's shuddery exhalation of relief. "Yeah. There. Not a millimeter lower, all right?"

"All...right."

The previous thrum in Callie's body accelerated to a barely throttled throb. She wasn't going to survive this without disgracing herself, she thought desperately. She just plain wasn't. Any split second now she was going to reveal herself as a totally wanton woman. And she was going to do it at high noon on a Sunday in the middle of the family's driveway!

Why in the name of heaven had she ever let Jake Turner talk her into getting on his damned Harley-Davidson with him?

Jake glanced back at her and grinned. There was a wicked gleam in his eyes. "Ready?" he asked.

All Callie could do was nod.

The day was hot and lazy.

The lovers were hot and rushed.

About all that stood between them and what they wanted were a few layers of clothing and a motel room door.

"Jake." Callie's tone was as aggravated as it was urgent. She had long since passed the point where she could exercise moderation around this man. While she'd disciplined herself to hide the emotions he evoked in her, she made no effort to disguise the appetites he aroused when they were together. "Jake, *please.*"

Jake swore. His heart was hammering. His temples throbbed. His sex felt as though it was encased in an iron glove that was two sizes too small and shrinking fast. He'd been fantasizing about carrying Callie off for a very private, very passionate afternoon at the Roadside Retreat

Motel for weeks and today he'd finally decided to stop dreaming and do it. The lady in question had been more than amenable to the idea. Fulfillment awaited.

And it was going to go on waiting if he couldn't get the damned door open!

"Jake, what's wrong?"

"This—" he cursed "—key isn't working."

"Try jiggling it." Callie leaned over to offer some assistance. She missed her intended point of contact by a country mile.

"I—*Callie!*" Jake filled his lungs with humid August air in a single shuddering inhalation. He got a good whiff of Callie's warm, womanly fragrance as he did so. Her scent was the essence of provocation, and it had very little to do with perfume. "For God's sake, sweetheart! I'm doing this the best way I know how."

"Forget the best way," she answered a little wildly. "Try the *fastest.*"

Jake gave a ragged laugh, fully understanding her frustration. He briefly contemplated trying an encore of the door-kicking performance that had altered his life some two decades before.

"He gave you the wrong key, didn't he?" Callie pushed a lock of hair back from her face with a not quite steady hand.

"What?" Jake rattled the door knob with barely restrained violence.

"That man at the front desk. The one who was dressed like Elvis Presley and sounded like Porky Pig. He gave you the wrong key!"

"I don't—" There was a sudden click of release as the key engaged in the lock. Jake welcomed the sound as though it signified the swinging open of the Pearly Gates. "Got it!"

Approximately a second and a half later Jake slammed the door of room four of the Roadside Retreat Motel shut and shoved the dead bolt home. Approximately a second and a half after that, Callie was in his arms and pressed up against the self-same door.

"Oh, sweetheart," he said thickly. "Oh...sweetheart."

"Y-yes," she responded shakily. "Oh, yes..."

Jake caged Callie's head between his hands, his fingers tangling irrevocably in her wavy hair. He brought his mouth down on hers, the bold thrust of his tongue between her lips both invasive and intimate. There were several dizzying moments of catch and cling when he forgot how to breathe.

The door at Callie's back was hard. Jake was even harder. She could feel the rigidity of his need and it thrilled her. She met and matched his kiss, her tongue slick and sinuous as it moved moistly over his. She stroked her hands down the lean length of his torso, then tugged at his T-shirt, hungry to touch his tautly muscled strength.

A shudder of desire racked him as her fingers found his skin. Continuing to hold Callie's head captive with one hand, Jake slid his other downward, insinuating it between their bodies. He undid the small pearl buttons on the blouse she was wearing with more force than finesse.

The catch on the front of her bra gave way a split second later.

Callie gasped as Jake's faintly callused fingers began to explore her newly bared breasts. She felt her nipples stiffen into tight rosettes. The whisper-light scrape of his nails against her tender flesh produced sensations so intense they were close to being torture.

His mouth left hers, kissing a path across to her right ear. He nipped gently at the soft lobe. He detailed his erotic intentions in dark velvet whispers, his heated breath fanning her skin. Callie shivered in expectation and acquiescence.

She located the snap at the top of his low-riding jeans by touch and jerked it open. A moment later, she pulled down the zipper of Jake's fly. A moment after that, she stroked the pulsing root of his masculine desire.

The hand that had been caressing her breasts moved lower still. The hem of the skirt she was wearing went one way, the lace-trimmed underwear beneath went the other.

"Callie—"

"Yes. Oh, yes."

Jake lifted her in a powerful movement. Callie arched up, offering herself. She cried out as he filled her, locking her legs around his hips, twining her arms around his neck.

The world seemed to stop for the space of a heartbeat. Existence was a matter of searing stillness, of sizzling suspension. And then they began to move together, perfectly attuned, ecstatically partnered.

"Oh...oh..." Callie arched a second time and then a third.

"So...beautiful..." Jake said hoarsely. He was on fire. Brain and body, he was burning. "Never...kn-knew..."

She sobbed out his name.

He invoked hers on a shattered breath.

In the end Callie Barnwell shared everything she had with Jake Turner except the ultimate truth—that she loved him and always would.

Jake looked up as he heard a muffled thud come from overhead. Work on the attic of the Quarter Oaks mansion had begun that morning. While the crew appeared to be expert, they obviously didn't believe in noise abatement. It sounded as though walls were tumbling down.

Maybe they were. Jake had gotten a look at the attic renovation plans and they were elaborate. Unfortunately the decision to do the job had been reached long after the other heavy duty interior work had been performed. This had injected an unnecessary bit of chaos into an already complicated project. Still, what Mr. Ichiai wanted, Mr. Ichiai got, and he apparently wanted a completely redone attic with the same intensity he'd wanted hand-carved mahogany moldings and custom-crafted cabinetry.

Jake wiped a forearm across his perspiration-sheened brow and surveyed the surface he'd been laboring over. Finishing was an integral part of the woodworking process and it couldn't be rushed. While he'd already made effective use of an orbital sander, the final stages had to be done by hand.

Frowning, he flexed his fingers, then cracked his knuckles. He'd methodically worked his way from a relatively rough-grit sandpaper to the finest available, carefully raising the softer grains of the wood with water-dampened sponge between passes. He was now polishing with steel wool, unlocking the wood's subtle but distinctive variations in tone in advance of staining. That staining, like the sanding, would be done with painstaking, hands-on precision, just the way Sam Swayze had taught him.

And once the staining was done...

Jake shook his head. In three days—four at the most—he would be finished with this project. It'd be all over but the paycheck. In five days, he would be gone from Deacon's Crossing. Right on schedule. Exactly as planned. He'd be on his way back to Vermont and a first-class plane ticket for a nine-day trip to England.

The problem was, a part of him didn't want to go.

That "part" was a facet of his nature he wasn't sure how to fight, because he'd never dealt with it before. Hell, he'd never even been aware of its existence! He wasn't certain whether it was something that had lain quiescent within him for decades or whether it had come into being since his arrival at Deacon's Crossing.

Just a few extra days, he thought. He'd been bargaining with himself about this matter for nearly a week now, and he'd yet to strike a deal. Just another week. Then I'll leave. They wouldn't mind. Miss Henny and P.D. wouldn't mind. And Callie...Callie wouldn't mind, either. She'd understand.

Wouldn't she?

"I'm leaving at the end of the month," he'd reminded her the fateful night Buttercup had given birth. *"I'm leaving and not coming back."*

And then afterward—after they'd made love—she'd assured him that he hadn't and wouldn't hurt her.

"You've been honest with me," she'd said as they'd lain together in a tangle of bed sheets. *"Now let me be honest with you. I know exactly what we can have together. I know*

exactly how long we can have it. And I want it, Jake. I want it all.''

But *all* on whose terms? he wondered suddenly. His? Hers?

Theirs?

Supposing he decided to act on this inexplicable impulse to stick around Deacon's Crossing for a while longer—to extend his lease with the Barnwells, so to speak. How would he explain himself to Callie? Would he tell her that the "all" they'd had hadn't been quite enough...that he wanted a little more?

Would he tell her that he'd like to delay the inevitable?

Because his leaving *was* inevitable. That was one of the few things Jake accepted absolutely. He knew himself far too well to do anything else.

He'd thought he knew Callie Barnwell, too. Practically from the moment they'd met, he'd had her pegged and pigeonholed as a woman to stay away from. Partly for his sake, but for hers as well. She obviously wasn't what Sam Swayze had once bluntly described as "a come-and-go lady."

But he hadn't stayed away from her. He'd gotten close to Callie. Very, very close. And, so far, the kinds of personal catastrophes he'd learned to associate with such intimacy hadn't happened. On the contrary, everything seemed to be working out perfectly.

Maybe that was at the root of the edginess that had been gnawing at him as his departure date approached. Maybe he didn't want things to be so perfect. Maybe he wanted to have a disastrous break with Callie in order to prove that his instincts about their incompatibility had been right. On the other hand, maybe he wanted her to give him some small sign that she—

"Yo, Jake!"

Jake started and turned toward the source of this basso profundo salutation.

"Yeah, Mal?" he asked the burly black man who was standing in the doorway of the oak-paneled library where he was working.

Mal grinned, wiping a ham-sized hand down the front of a sweat-stained khaki T-shirt. "You the big expert on the history of this house, right?"

Jake grimaced. Somehow, the tiny part he'd played in getting Quarter Oaks' original name restored had gotten blown way out of proportion. Although Callie had kept quiet about what he'd done, Augustus Bates had dug up the details and printed them in the *Deacon's Crossing Weekly*. This had triggered an embarrassing—although not altogether unpleasant—outpouring of gratitude from Miss Henny as well as some ribbing around the work site.

"Yeah, Mal," he answered wryly. "I'm doing a dissertation on it."

"Well, dissertate on what we just uncovered up in the attic."

"What is it?"

"Good question, man. Come on and check it out."

"Callie, dear, what do *you* think?" Petal Conroy demanded.

Callie stared at her aunt's best friend for several seconds, guiltily aware that she'd been ignoring the conversation going on around her. She was also aware that such a social lapse would not sit well with Petal Conroy.

Callie had not anticipated finding the president of the Historical Preservation Society of Deacon's Crossing ensconced in the parlor when she arrived home from her shop. She'd tried to excuse herself after a brief exchange of greetings, but Petal Conroy wouldn't have it.

"Ah...what do I think about what, Miz Conroy?" she asked tentatively.

Petal Conroy gave her a look which, according to local legend, was capable of stopping a clock at fifty paces.

"This feud your aunt is conductin' with Augustus Bates."

Callie glanced around. She very dimly recalled hearing her aunt raise an objection to the fact that Augustus Bates had been invited to serve as master of ceremonies for the historical portion of the Founders' Day Festival program.

"Well, I'm sure Aunt Henny has her reasons..."

"I'm sure she does, too," Petal Conroy snapped. "But after huggin' them to her bosom for more than forty years, I'd've thought she'd've squeezed them dry!"

"Forty years?" Callie began, giving her aunt a startled look.

"Petal Conroy, I will thank you not to wash my personal laundry in public," Henny interrupted stiffly. "And I am not feudin' with Augustus Bates. Why, I hardly know the man's alive most of the—"

"Lord, now what is *that?*" Petal Conroy cut in abruptly, cocking her head.

The "that", Callie realized with a sudden leap of her heart, was the sound of Jake Turner's Harley-Davidson. She said as much.

"You mean that Yankee you've had livin' with you? The one who talked that Japanese fella—Itchy-choo—into callin' Quarter Oaks Quarter Oaks again? You know, Callie, just the other day at the beauty parlor my manicurist told me that her cousin's brother-in-law's sister's son saw you out ridin' around on the back of that motor-sicle of his. But I told her I just couldn't believe—"

"Callie?" Jake's strong male voice rang out from the front hallway.

"In here," Callie called, getting to her feet.

A moment later Jake appeared in the doorway of the parlor. He was holding an untidy bundle wrapped in what appeared to be oilcloth and twine.

"This is for you," he announced without preamble, moving forward.

"What—?" Callie asked uncertainly as Jake practically thrust the bundle into her hands.

"It's from the attic at Quarter Oaks. I think it's Caroline Anne Barnwell's wedding dress."

Ten

_____

"I know it's only been two days since the momentous discovery, Callie," Henrietta Barnwell said, patting her mouth with a napkin. "But are you almost done designin'? I swear, I've gotten so many phone calls from members of the Historical Preservation Society wantin' to know how it's comin', my ear's like to fall off any second."

"I think the design will be finished tomorrow, Aunt Henny," Callie replied, toying with the food on her supper plate. She glanced across the table at Jake, noting that he, too, had barely touched his meal. He hadn't spoken for the last few minutes, either.

"It's goin' to be so touchin'!" the older woman gushed. "You readin' from Caroline Anne's diaries while wearin' a re-creation of her weddin' dress made out of material from the original. You just wait. People will be sobbin' up a storm when you reach the line about white lace promises."

Callie suppressed a small sigh. She'd been hearing variations on this theme for the past forty-eight hours. It had started moments after Jake's dramatic presentation of the find from the attic at Quarter Oaks. Petal Conroy had grasped the possibilities immediately and proceeded accordingly. Her initial edict—issued with the full authority vested in the president of the Historical Preservation Society—had been that Callie must wear the original gown during the Founders' Day Festival. This order had been retracted in favor of the "re-creation" scheme after an inspection of the garment revealed that it had been made for a woman who stood no more than five-foot-one and had a twenty-inch waist.

"Well, as I've been telling everyone who's dropped by the shop to take a look, it's not going to be an exact re-creation," Callie cautioned her aunt. "I'm trying to capture the spirit of the gown, not do a line-by-line copy."

"Speakin' of spirits," P.D. interpolated through a mouthful of half-chewed butter beans. "Me and Seth Avery were talkin' about the possibility that Callie dressin' like Caroline Anne might stir up Harriman Gage's ghost. 'Magine him puttin' in an appearance at the Founders' Day Festival?"

"Oh, hush, P.D.," Henny returned with a tinge of exasperation. "We're discussin' something deeply movin' and meaningful here. There's no call for you draggin' the ghost of Harriman Gage into it."

The teenager took this gentle scolding in stride. He glanced at Jake. "Bet you'd stick around if you thought old Harriman was goin' to come back from the grave," he observed disingenuously.

Jake responded with a wordless gesture that fell somewhere between confirmation and denial of this possibility.

There was a brief pause. For several moments the only sounds at the table were the soft clink of cutlery against china and the rather noisy gnashing of P.D.'s teeth.

"More stuffin', Jacob?" Henny inquired eventually.

"No, thank you, Miss Henny," Jake refused politely, setting down his fork. Although he'd put in a long day at the Quarter Oaks work site, he had very little appetite... for food.

"That sweet Stella Avery brought it over earlier," the older woman remarked. "She said she'd made up an extra big batch and didn't want it goin' to waste. Wasn't that thoughtful of her?"

"She must've been rehearsin' her onstage talent for the pageant again," P.D. commented with a snicker. He wolfed down a biscuit, then took a giant gulp of milk from the glass at his elbow. "She's got this rubber chicken she practices with, tryin' to get the timin' just right. Seth says they've been eatin' so much stuffin' at his house lately he's about to bust his gut!"

"Palmer Dean Barnwell the Third, I simply won't abide that kind of vulgar talk!" Henny said. "First ghosts, now guts! Stuffin' and bustin', indeed. And where are your table manners? I declare, you've been behavin' like a half-starved hog all through supper. You'd think you hadn't had a bite to eat in a month of Sundays. Is that how you want Jacob to remember you?"

The teenager ducked his head, looking properly chastised. "No," he muttered. "Sorry, Aunt Henny."

"Fine," his aunt responded with a gracious nod. She served herself a dainty dollop of Stella's stuffing, then turned her attention back to Jake. "I do apologize for P.D.," she said.

"No problem," Jake responded. He looked across the table at Callie. She was contemplating a pair of butter beans she'd impaled on the tines of her fork. Her expression was abstracted and more than a little aloof.

Apparently sensing his scrutiny, Callie suddenly shifted her focus from her fork to him. Her mouth tipped upward at the corners in a smile that didn't quite touch her eyes. Jake felt a strange tightening in his chest.

"You *sure* you have to leave on Saturday, Jake?" P.D. asked abruptly, reverting to a subject he'd been bringing up at increasingly frequent intervals during the past few days. "Founders' Day's just a little over two weeks away. And by that time, Buttercup's puppies will be big enough so you can have one. Can't you stay till then?"

Jake looked at the teenager, then back at Callie. She'd put down her fork and was watching him with a serene expression.

Ask me to stay until the festival, Callie, he thought. *Ask me to stay and I will. Just give me a hint that's what you want.*

Callie turned to her half brother. "Jake's got places to go and people to see, P.D.," she said quietly. "He has commitments. And he travels too much to take care of a pet. So stop pestering him. He came to Deacon's Crossing for two months and those two months are up the day after tomorrow."

Henny heaved a sigh. "Let's just hope Jacob's departure is less eventful than his arrival. I don't think I could bear another shotgun blast."

Callie was dreaming she was dressed in white lace.

A soft spill of it—as insubstantial as a shadow—veiled her head.

A luxurious length of it—as intricate as a spider's web—draped her body.

"Callie?" A whisper.

She could feel the teasing texture of the delicate material against her skin. She could hear the subtle rustle of it as she moved.

"Callie?" Still a whisper, but more intense.

Now the lace was being lifted away, gently eased aside. Faintly callused fingertips brushed her newly bared flesh, sending quicksilver heat rippling through her. She wanted...she wanted...

"Callie?" Beyond intense, approaching urgency.

Callie awoke with a muffled cry. Her eyes fluttered open and she found herself staring up into Jake Turner's face.

"Shhh, sweetheart," he murmured, gently stroking his knuckles down her cheek. "It's just me. Jake."

"J-Jake?" she echoed unsteadily. She started to lever herself up into a sitting position. Glancing toward the clock on the small stand next to her bed, she saw that it was a few minutes after eleven. "Is something wrong?"

Jake shook his head. "Everything's fine," he answered, keeping his voice low.

"Then what—?"

He stole the question she was about to ask with a swift kiss.

"Oh, Jake," Callie breathed when he lifted his lips from hers. She raised one hand and rubbed her fingers against his jaw, feeling the sandpapery hint of new beard growth. She knew he shouldn't be in her bedroom. They'd agreed that this kind of encounter was too risky. "Please..."

"I want to be with you tonight, Callie," he said with devastating simplicity.

Jake started to dip his head to kiss her again. She used her hand to restrain him.

"We can't," she said, hearing a yearning note in her voice that clearly revealed how much she wished they could. Jake was due to leave in the morning. It would mean everything to her if they could spend these final hours together.

"Yes, we can," he argued, capturing her hand and kissing the back of it. "I've got a plan."

"A plan?"

Jake nodded.

Callie's pulse accelerated. She moistened her lips. "What kind of plan?"

"Come with me," was all he said.

She did.

"So, Callie?" Jake questioned with a lazy smile about an hour later. "What do you think of my plan?"

"Amazing," Callie responded with absolute candor. What other word could she use to describe a plan that had involved whisking her off on a motorcycle for a moonlight swim at Flat Rock Pond? she wondered.

It was a perfect night. A study in serenity. Stars winked in the sky like diamonds set against lush, ink-blue velvet. The moon glowed fat and full, imbuing everything it touched with an iridescent enchantment. The pond held the heady warmth of a string of sizzling summer days.

Callie knew she would remember this beautiful, bittersweet time with aching clarity for the rest of her life.

They were treading water about five yards apart, their movements smooth and subtle. Jake could see Callie quite clearly thanks to the moon's ethereal glow. Her wet hair was slicked back from her face, emphasizing both the delicacy and strength of her features. Her expression held a delicious hint of mischief.

"Glad you came?" he asked.

Callie laughed throatily. "Guess," she challenged.

"Give me a hint," he countered.

Callie cocked her head to one side, pretended to ponder the idea. Then, after a few teasing seconds, she swam over to him. In the interim, Jake planted his feet on the bottom of the pond and stood up. The water reached his breastbone.

Following his example, Callie stood up, too. The water lapped softly at her shoulders as she studied the man she loved but couldn't tell. The moonlight transformed Jake's face into a striking amalgam of shadows and highlights. It endowed him with a provocative, almost pagan, aura. She saw his lips part and his teeth glint white, as though he relished her open scrutiny of him.

"Well?" she murmured. "What do you think?"

"What do I think about...what?" Jake returned, losing the thread of their conversation. Moonlight at midnight flattered Callie in an almost magical way. The skin of her shoulders, throat, cheeks and brow gleamed as though it had been polished with powdered pearls. Her eyes were dark and dreamy.

A bead of water trembled at one corner of her mouth. It glinted like a drop of molten silver. Jake watched Callie's tongue dart out and lick it away. He felt his body stir and stiffen.

Callie smiled fleetingly. "About whether I'm glad to be here."

"I certainly hope you are."

She smiled again. The curve that reshaped her lips lingered this time. "I'm more than glad," she answered softly.

There was a fractional pause. Then Jake issued a boldly simple invitation.

"Show me," he said.

He clasped Callie gently when she came within touching distance, gathering her close. He stroked his hands slowly down her back, briefly cupping her bottom. As his hands slid to her thighs, her legs came up to wrap around his hips.

Callie moved her body languidly against Jake's. She was completely naked. He had on a pair of cotton briefs. The single layer of stretchy fabric did nothing to mute her awareness of the heated hardness of his arousal. Soon, she promised herself, rubbing her hands against his broad chest. Very soon.

Jake caught his breath as Callie found his nipples. She circled the hard bits of male flesh with her nails, then plucked at them very delicately. Twin lightning bolts of excitement arrowed directly down to his groin. Jake thought for several searing seconds that he was going to lose control. Not yet, he warned himself fiercely. Not...quite...yet.

Callie angled her head to the right, circling Jake's neck with her arms. She nipped lightly at the lobe of his left ear, relishing the tremor of response she felt run through him. After a few seconds she licked the places where she had bitten.

"Aren't you worried that someone might see us?" she whispered.

Jake chuckled deep in his throat. "Here? At this time of night?"

"But if *we're* up..."

There was no *if* in this case, Jake reflected. He definitely was up. He altered his embrace of Callie just a little. The feel of her sweet, womanly weight was almost more than he could endure.

"I think we're safe from prying eyes," he told her. "There are trees all around, and this pond is a mile from the nearest road." He brushed his mouth against hers once... twice... then kissed his way up to her ear. "We're all alone," he murmured with dark intensity. "Just you and me."

"Just you... and me," Callie echoed, shivering when he nipped at her earlobe the way she had nibbled on his only moments before. She shifted instinctively, caressing Jake's strong body with her soft one.

"Oh, sweetheart," he said raggedly, his fingers tightening against her. "Do you have any idea what you're doing to me?"

She answered him with a smile that could have originated with Eve.

Jake invoked her name on a guttural growl.

Callie shook her head, then touched her mouth to his. Their breaths married for an instant. Their tongues mated.

"Make love with me, Jake," she invited in a husky whisper when the kiss finally came to an end. Her voice held both plea and provocation. "Make love with me now."

Jake needed no additional urging.

He changed his hold on Callie, gripping her firmly with his left arm. Freeing his right hand, he slid it slowly from her breast to her hip, then slipped it between her legs. He caressed the triangle of springy hair at the juncture of her thighs, then sought the soft, silken heat of her inner flesh. He eased into her very slowly. He felt a split second of reflexive tightening at the intrusion followed by an unmistakable opening.

Callie said his name, her lashes fluttering down, her throat arching back. The water of the pond licked at her feminine secrets, creating an erotic counterpoint to the loving stroke of Jake's lean fingers. A quiver of pleasure danced up her spine. Her breath unraveled in a shuddery thread of sound as she spoke his name again.

"Look at me, Callie," Jake said.

After a few seconds, Callie did. Her eyelids felt heavy, her skin flushed.

Jake let his gaze rove over her upturned face, gauging the heat in her cheeks and the hunger in her eyes. "I want you so much," he told her, his fingers continuing to arouse and ready her.

"I want you, too," she answered. She wished from the bottom of her heart she dared substitute the word that described her true feelings for the man who was ravishing her senses with his secret, rhythmic touch, but she knew it was impossible. Jake Turner didn't expect her love. More than that, he wouldn't accept it.

And he certainly wouldn't offer his own in return.

Callie trailed one hand down Jake's chest to his flat belly, then moved lower still. Slowly, deliberately, she slid her fingers beneath the waistband of his briefs. Just as slowly, just as deliberately, she cupped the blunt length of his potency in her palm and eased it free of all constraint. She saw his features grow taut, his eyes turn dark.

"Callie." Her name left his lips on a hiss of breath. He moved his hips. Her hand clasped him in the most intimate fashion imaginable, guiding him to the place he ached to be.

"Yes," she told him. "Yes... now. All of you."

The urge to sheathe himself hard and to the hilt was very strong. But Jake fought it down. Instead he took Callie by inches, penetrating her in ruthlessly measured increments. She inhaled on a series of staccato gasps as he filled her, then exhaled on a melting sigh when his possession was complete.

"Oh... oh, Jake..."

Jake groaned, trembling with the effort it took to restrain himself. The feel of Callie's body around his was the most intensely erotic thing he'd ever experienced. He groaned a second time when she rocked her pelvis against him.

"No," he said, his voice grating against the soft silence of the night. "Please, Callie." His lips pulled back from gritted teeth. "Don't. Please... don't move."

"I can't—"

"Please. Just for..." He kissed her lips, her nose, her temples. His fingers spasmed against her hips, holding her fast. "Just for a few seconds. Being inside you like this...sweetheart. I want...I want it to last a little longer."

Callie gave Jake the few seconds he'd asked for. Then, driven by ancient appetites she could no longer resist, she tightened her legs, taking him even deeper into the core of her womanhood.

"Callie! Oh, God," Jake groaned for a third time, a shudder of pleasure racking him from top to toe. He felt as though he was being caressed by a glove made of burning satin. Any moment now he was going to explode. He could feel the pulsating urge for consummation building within him.

"Yes," Callie said, her breath coming in tight, quick pants, her lashes fluttering down once again. *"Yes."*

Ecstasy was approaching like a white-hot wave. Callie could hear its roar in her ears. She could see its shimmering beauty behind her tightly closed eyelids. She tried to brace herself for the moment it broke over her.

But there was no way of preparing for the first onslaught of pleasure that surged up within her. It was like nothing she'd ever experienced, ever imagined. It engulfed her with a wild, wanton force, buffeting every fiber of her being. Callie clung to Jake, sobbing his name over and over, trying not to drown in the seething sea of sensations she and her lover of one month had unleashed.

Jake couldn't think. Couldn't breathe. He tried to say Callie's name, but the two syllables left his lips in fragments. Reality narrowed to thrust and throb, to skin against skin, mouth against mouth.

Release, when they ultimately reached it, was simultaneous and shattering. It obliterated all differences and fused them body and soul.

"Mmm..." Callie sighed, running a fingertip lightly down Jake's right forearm, tracing the sinews beneath the sun-darkened skin.

"Yeah," Jake responded, nuzzling his lips gently against her damp hair.

Nearly two hours had elapsed since their ecstatic merging at Flat Rock Pond. They'd arrived back at the Barnwell house on Jake's motorcycle a short while before. They were still sitting on the Harley, he clad in his usual jeans and white T-shirt, she dressed in the deceptively demure nightgown she'd been wearing when he'd lured her out of bed. But their positions were far different than they'd been when they'd been riding. As soon as he'd parked the motorcycle, Jake had shifted Callie's body, bringing her forward and cradling her in his lap.

He hadn't really thought about what he was doing until he'd done it, and once he'd thought about it, he'd felt more than a little unsettled. As uninhibited as he was during lovemaking, Jake had always shied from intimacies in the aftermath of it. Callie was the first woman he'd ever known who inspired him to cuddle. Looking back, he realized it had been that way from the first. Instead of automatically easing away from her after the act, he'd wanted to prolong the closeness between them. And not just physically, either. No, he'd felt an urge to talk as well as touch.

Jake inhaled deeply through his nose, then released the breath through his lips on a hissing sigh.

You're leaving, he reminded himself. You're leaving later today and it's the best thing for all concerned. You know that.

"Jake?" Callie questioned, twisting so she could look up at him. "What's wrong?"

"Nothing," he said, instinctively evading her gaze by glancing toward the front of the house. "Just...thinking."

Callie scrutinized his angular face. It was impossible to decipher what lay behind his enigmatic expression, but she thought she caught a flicker of the sadness she herself was feeling. Was it possible he regretted his impending departure? she asked herself. Was it possible he didn't want to leave?

Words rose in her throat. Words of longing. Words of love. Callie swallowed hard, forcing them down. She had no right to utter such words and she knew it. One month was what she'd asked for. Agreed to. And one month—one glorious month—was what she'd received.

"Thinking about what?" she asked after a few moments. The sadness, if sadness was what she'd seen, was gone from Jake's features.

Jake searched for an appropriate answer. For an answer that wouldn't require explanations he didn't know how to make to anyone, including himself. A window on the second floor of the house provided him with inspiration.

"I'm thinking about the first time I saw you," he said.

Callie made a rueful sound. "When I came charging down the stairs in my economy-sized T-shirt, you mean?"

"Before that."

"*Before* that?"

"Right after I pulled up in my truck. I saw you there," he pointed. "Silhouetted against the window of your bedroom."

Callie frowned, recalling the night in question. She'd worked late in her shop, then arrived home to an excited announcement from her Aunt Henny that a prospective tenant was on the way. So, she'd trooped upstairs to change her—

"Oh," she said in a muffled voice, feeling her face go pink with embarrassment. "I can't imagine what you must have thought."

Jake chuckled. "Oh, I'd imagine you could if you put your mind to it. You've gotten to know me pretty well during the past eight weeks."

Callie managed a crooked smile. "Did you think that the woman in the window was your type?" she asked. Even though she knew the question was unwise, she couldn't stop herself from voicing it.

Jake felt something twist inside him. Was that reproach he heard coloring Callie's words? Was it regret? Or was it another emotion he couldn't—or wouldn't—identify?

He stroked a hand down one of Callie's bare arms. "Let's just say I thought I wanted to find out," he answered after a few seconds.

Callie wasn't certain how to respond to this, so she didn't. After a brief pause she asked, "Why didn't you tell me?"

"About seeing you in the window?"

She nodded.

Jake circled her wrist with his fingers. "Well, it's not the sort of thing I could just drop into a conversation," he replied wryly.

There was another brief pause. After a few moments Jake dropped a light kiss on Callie's brow.

"And speaking of not telling," he resumed reflectively. "Why didn't you tell me the truth about Caroline Barnwell and Harriman Gage?"

Callie stiffened. "I did."

"Not the whole truth. You never told me he drowned."

"Oh . . . well . . ." She made a little gesture.

"You know, I had old Harriman pegged for a complete lowlife before Augustus Bates set me straight."

Callie manufactured a laugh. This subject was extremely uncomfortable for her. The last thing she wanted to do right now was to think about an ancestress who had loved and lost.

"Don't let Aunt Henny hear you say that," she advised. "I don't think she could stand the idea of Augustus Bates telling anyone about our family history."

"Probably not," Jake conceded.

There was another pause, this one longer than the two before.

"It's getting late," Callie murmured finally.

"Actually, it's getting early," Jake amended. "It'll be dawn before too long."

"You need to get some sleep before you leave."

"Yeah. Right."

"Well, then . . ." Callie started to disengage from Jake's embrace.

He held her fast. "Callie."

Her heart lurched at his tone. "What?"

"What are white lace promises?"

Callie had to swallow hard. "White lace promises?" she repeated.

"I remember Stella Avery used that phrase weeks ago in your shop. And your aunt said it again tonight."

"It's from Caroline Anne's diary," she explained after a moment. "The day she came out of the attic at Quarter Oaks—oh, did Mr. Bates tell you about that?"

Jake nodded.

"Well, she wrote nearly five pages on that day. And part of what she wrote is about white lace promises."

"About them being broken?"

"No, not really." Callie veiled her eyes with her lashes, then recited, "'And so, I will put away my dreams of white lace promises and devote myself to doing good. Although my heart and my arms may be empty, my life will be filled with charity for others.'"

"Sad."

"Very," she agreed, lifting her lashes to meet Jake's compelling gaze once again.

"Callie—" he started, his tone and features taut.

Callie shook her head quickly. She read guilt in Jake's expression, heard guilt in his voice. That was the last thing she wanted him to feel now or after they parted. There was no reason for it.

"No," she said softly, putting her fingertips to his mouth. "Don't. I'm not Caroline Anne Barnwell and you're not Harriman Gage. What we've had this last month...it was never a matter of white lace promises, Jake. I know that. You know that."

Jake stayed silent for several seconds, wondering whether the emotion churning inside him was relief or resentment at how easy Callie was making it for him. He remembered the times he'd tried to explain the difference between them by telling her she was hello and he was goodbye. It suddenly occurred to him that he'd underestimated her flair for farewells.

For reasons he couldn't articulate and didn't particularly want to examine, this notion hurt.

"Yeah, Callie," Jake concurred tersely. "We both know it."

And then he kissed her.

He kissed her again less than eight hours later, just before he got into his pickup and drove away.

Eleven

One week after the departure of the man she loved, Callie Barnwell stood in front of a full-length mirror trying not to cry. She was clad in an elegantly old-fashioned gown made of satin and lace. The lace was more than a century old. The satin had been purchased in Atlanta just five days earlier.

A mistake, she thought miserably. This was a mistake.

She still wasn't sure why she'd consented to give Stella Avery and Janie Mae Winslow an advanced peek at her re-creation of Caroline Anne Barnwell's wedding gown. The two young women had arrived at Callie's Corner shortly before closing time, then refused to leave until she showed them what they desperately wanted to see.

Had it been just Janie Mae, Callie most likely would have stood firm in her resolve to keep the dress hidden until it was completely finished. Unfortunately the pleading expression in Stella's eyes had undermined her determination. In the end she'd capitulated and retreated to the dressing room where she was now. Janie Mae and Stella had elected to remain out front, where they'd become involved in a discussion of proper pageant deportment.

"You've got to remember your string, Stella," Janie Mae was insisting.

"But I don't have a string, Janie Mae." Stella sounded deeply distressed by this deficiency.

"Of *course* you have a string! Every aspirin' beauty has one. It's comin' right out of the top of our skull and it's attached to a big golden balloon filled with helium."

"But—"

"Stella, just close your eyes and feel the string!" There was a brief pause. "That's right. That's right. Just feel that old string drawin' you up...up...up till you're standin' with perfect queenly posture."

Tears pricked at the corners of Callie's eyes as she stared into the mirror. It was obvious from her reflection that her posture was anything but regal at the moment. She blinked hard. Her lips shaped the name of the man who had taken her heart without realizing it was in his possession.

Jake, she thought yearningly. Oh, Jake.

"It this better, Janie Mae?" The inquiry was hopeful.

"Well, it's an improvement over that pitiful slump you were in a few minutes ago," came the uncompromising response. "Now, pull your shoulders back and try to throw out your baz—oh, never mind that. Suck in your stomach and tuck your tailbone under. Come on, Stella. Suck and tuck!"

"Janie Mae...oh, Janie Mae...this doesn't feel very comfortable."

"Beauty knows no pain. Why, if I told you the agony I went through with my electrolysis, you'd just want to curl up and die."

Callie bit her lip. Pain. It had been her constant companion ever since she'd waved goodbye to Jake. Not physical pain, but close to it. She was haunted by an aching sense of loss. She'd spent the past seven days struggling to survive in an awful, empty void.

You knew, she reminded herself fiercely, adjusting the puffed sleeves of her gown. Struggling for control, she took a deep breath. A half dozen straight pins stabbed into her. You knew from the very beginning he was going to leave you.

Callie exhaled on a heavy sigh.

Yes, she'd known. But what she hadn't realized was how much it was going to hurt!

You told Jake it was all right, she continued. You told him you knew you'd only have a month and you didn't care.

Yes, she'd told him. And in doing so, she'd perjured herself, heart and soul.

"Now, I want you to try to take a few glidin' steps forward, Stella," Janie Mae declared. "And, when you do, I want you to pretend you've got a silver dollar tucked between your cheeks."

"My...my cheeks, Janie Mae?"

"Not those cheeks! I'm talkin' your behind!"

Callie knuckled the pale skin of her face, then fiddled with the small bustle at the back of her gown. That done, she drew herself up, ignoring the pins that pricked in a dozen different places. After a moment she squared her shoulders and reached for the dressing room curtain.

She emerged just in time to see Stella start to execute a pageant-style pivot. The reed-thin blonde did fine for the first 180 degrees of the turn, then her feet got tangled up.

"Stella!" Callie gasped.

Something—maybe it was the string she allegedly had coming out of the top of her skull—enabled Stella to regain her balance. She certainly got no help from Janie Mae Winslow. The buxom brunette didn't move a muscle to assist. However, her mouth did drop open when she turned her head and saw Callie.

"It's all right. It's all—" Stella broke off and stared.

"Well?" Callie asked, lifting her chin slightly. She glanced back and forth between the two young women she was confronting.

"Oh, Callie," Stella sighed. "Oh, Callie, that's the most breathtakin' gown I've ever seen. You look so beautiful I could cry."

"Oh, don't do that," Janie Mae retorted snippily. "There's absolutely nothin' uglier than mascara streaks."

The blonde eyed the brunette. "Don't you think Callie looks beautiful?"

Janie Mae fluffed her dark hair. "What? With those horrible dark circles under her eyes?" she responded. "I swear, Callie, you look like you haven't slept a wink in a week. But don't worry. I know just the trick. A poultice of finely chopped cucumbers topped with soakin' tea bags."

For the first time in seven days, Callie laughed.

Three nights later, Callie cried. Sitting on the edge of her bed, she blotted her tears with a dirty white T-shirt that carried the scent of Jake Turner's skin.

She'd found the T-shirt in the laundry just a few hours after he'd driven away. She hadn't washed it. Instead she'd taken it upstairs and hidden it away in her bedroom. The inexpensive cotton garment was the only tangible legacy she had from the man she loved.

No. Not quite the only one. Jake had also left her his mailing address. He'd taped it to the refrigerator in the kitchen. There'd been no explanation offered. No indication that he expected—or wanted—her to stay in touch. Just a scrawled post office box number, the name of a town in Vermont and a zip code.

Callie could take little comfort from a slip of paper with an address on it. She couldn't hug it. She couldn't hold it against her and inhale a hint of male muskiness that triggered intimate memories of ecstasy. She couldn't even...

"Stop it!" Callie ordered herself in an angry undertone. "Just stop wallowing in self-pity! It's over. *Over.* You knew from the beginning it would be."

She drew a shuddery breath, calling on every ounce of self-discipline she had. She hated the way she was acting. She'd been strong for so many years in the face of so many things. But now she was buckling like soggy cardboard under an emotional burden that she had willingly chosen to bear.

"Better one month than none," she'd told herself the night she and Jake first made love. "Better remembrances of what was...than regrets about what might have been but never happened."

Callie had no regrets about what might have been. But, dear God, the remembrances of—

A knock at her bedroom door derailed this train of thought.

"Callie?"

Callie sniffed and hastily wiped her eyes with the T-shirt.

"Come in," she said, stuffing the garment beneath her pillow.

The door opened. Henrietta Barnwell entered on slippered feet. Her plump body was stiff beneath her blue chenille bathrobe. Her expression held a peculiar mixture of distress and determination.

"Aunt Henny?" Callie questioned warily.

The older woman closed the door. She stood silently for several seconds, the look on her face growing more and more conflicted.

"Aunt Henny?" Callie repeated, her wariness turning to worry. "What's wrong?"

Her aunt took a deep breath, clearly gathering her resolve.

"I can't stand it!" she burst out finally, crossing to the bed. "I've tried and I've tried, but I can't stand it!"

Callie blinked, startled. "What can't you stand?"

"Seein' you like this."

Callie pasted on a smile she hoped looked more convincing than it felt. "But I'm fine, Aunt Henny," she said. "Just fine."

"In a pig's eye you're just fine," the older woman retorted sharply, then sagged a little. She twisted her hands together. "You're dwindlin' away into spinsterhood just like every Barnwell daughter since the first Caroline Anne. It's been goin' on for more than a century now. You'd think the women in this family'd be due *some* luck in love after all these years. And I was so sure it was goin' to happen for you and Jacob!''

"M-me and—and Jake?" Callie stammered, feeling her cheeks flame. "What makes you think—"

"I don't *think*," her aunt interrupted. "I know. Why, the two of you started goin' off like firecrackers practically from the first moment you met. I swear, there were times you'd look at him and he'd look at you and the room would turn hotter than asphalt in August."

Callie gasped.

"Of course, I was worried about that awful fight you had the night P.D. snuck out and got himself all liquored up," the older woman continued with a grimace.

"You know about P.D. getting drunk?" Callie's voice was an octave above normal.

"Well, of course, I know about it! I may be gettin' on in years, Caroline Anne Barnwell, but I'm not deaf, blind, or stupid. When I get woken up in the middle of the night by the sound of my nephew desecratin' one of my favorite songs by Elvis Presley, it doesn't take much figurin' to deduce the cause of the situation. Still I thought it was best to stay put once I heard you go tearin' down the stairs and let fly at Jacob."

"You knew?" Callie couldn't believe it. She simply could not believe it. "All this time, you knew what happened that night and you didn't say anything?"

Henny cocked her chin. "I don't recall you mentionin' the episode, either," she pointed out.

Callie opened and closed her mouth several times. She supposed there had to be an appropriate response to this very valid observation but, for the life of her, she couldn't think of what it might be.

"As I said," her aunt resumed doggedly. "I was afraid that awful fight would end up doomin' my hopes. But I soon realized you and Jacob had had the good sense to make up with each other. Then I started thinkin' about how difficult it must be for the two of you to find any privacy what with me and P.D. underfoot, so I decided I had to do somethin' about it.''

Comprehension didn't dawn. It clouted Callie like a sledgehammer to the back of her head.

"Ohmigod," she gasped. "Oh...my...God. You went on that church outing to Atlanta on purpose!"

"Well, I certainly didn't go on it by accident," came the slightly nettled confirmation. "Not that I minded the opportunity to go shoppin' with Petal Conroy at one of those lovely malls. And I know P.D. enjoyed—"

"Oh, God! You didn't tell P.D. what you were trying to do!"

Henny rolled her eyes. "No, I didn't tell P.D. Although, to be perfectly honest, I think he may have had some suspicions."

Callie groaned and covered her face with her hands. After a moment she caught a faint whiff of lavender-scented talcum powder. A moment after that, she felt the mattress give as her aunt sat down next to her.

"There, there, child," the older woman said, patting her shoulder.

Callie lowered her hands and turned her head. "I'm not a child, Aunt Henny," she contradicted heavily. "I'm a thirty-year-old woman."

"I know. I know," her aunt clucked sympathetically. She waited a few seconds, then added, "A thirty-year-old woman who's breakin' her heart over the man she loves."

Callie caught her breath at the stark description. She wanted to deny it, but she knew it wouldn't work. Oh, she could lie with her lips, but the truth would be in her eyes for her aunt to see.

There was a painful pause.

"Did you tell Jacob you loved him?" Henny asked gently.

Callie flinched from the idea. "No!"

The older woman looked more sorrowful than shocked by the vehemence of this response. "Why not?"

"Because he didn't want to hear it, Aunt Henny! He— what we had—I mean, it wasn't—" Callie stopped, trying to find the right words. "I knew from the very start Jake wasn't going to stay. He never made any promises. He told me from the beginning that it wouldn't work. That we were two entirely different people. That I w-wasn't his type and he wasn't m-mine." She swallowed hard, despising the wobbliness in her voice. "What happened was my doing more than his. I...made up my mind I'd rather have one month with him than none."

The sorrow had drained away from Henny's features. In its place was an emotion Callie couldn't quite get a fix on.

"So you just let him go." Henny's tone was as difficult to interpret as her expression.

Callie gestured helplessly. "He was going to go no matter what I did."

"Are you sure of that?"

"Am I—? Of course, I'm sure! Didn't you listen to what I said? Didn't you hear the things he told me?"

"Yes, I heard." The older woman's eyes flashed. "And while I don't pretend to understand everythin' about the state of modern male-female relations, I do understand old-fashioned gumption. I always thought you had an abundant supply of that, Callie. Unfortunately it's becomin' painfully obvious to me that I was mistaken."

Callie was completely unprepared for this kind of attack. "What...what do you mean?" she managed to ask.

Her aunt—her normally placid, pleasant aunt—was more than ready to offer a point-by-point explanation.

"You love a man and you don't tell him," she declared. "You let him leave when you don't want him to go. And now you appear to be content to sit around and stew in your own juices like some human prune. If that doesn't demonstrate a lack of gumption, I don't know what does. And I happen to be somethin' of an expert on lack of g-gumption."

Henny's voice wavered on the last word. Then her lips began to tremble. Her throat worked visibly and her eyes sheened over with tears.

"Oh, d-damnation!" she said thickly. "It's history repeatin' itself all over again."

The abrupt transition from scolding to near sobbing left Callie completely confused. "Aunt Henny, please," she said, searching for something soothing to say. "My situation is nothing like Caroline Anne's."

"Oh, I wasn't talkin' about her," the older woman snapped. She sniffed loudly and dabbed at her eyes with the cuff of her bathrobe. "Although, if you really want to know, I've always believed that she was pretty spineless, too. Oh, I don't doubt that Harriman Gage's gettin' himself drowned the way he did cast a genuine blight on her existence. But to go lockin' herself in the attic for six months? And then to turn into a martyr to good works after she came out? Why, if that girl had had an ounce of spunk, she'd've done her mournin', then gone out and found another man."

Callie took a moment to try to digest this radical reinterpretation of Barnwell family history. The assessment proved to be much easier to swallow than she expected. What stuck in her craw was what her aunt had said before she'd veered onto the subject of Caroline Anne's lack of spine.

"Well, then," she began carefully, "if you weren't talking about Caroline Anne and Harriman Gage when you mentioned history repeating itself . . . who *were* you talking about?"

Henrietta Barnwell looked down. She studied her hands silently for nearly ten seconds, then slowly raised her eyes to meet Callie's.

"I was talkin' about me and Augustus Bates."

Callie realized she'd been holding her breath. She released it in a hiss. "You . . . and Augustus Bates?"

The older woman nodded. "It was a few years after World War Two. Augustus started courtin' me after a fashion. We had to see each other on the sly because my daddy and his daddy didn't get along." She grimaced. " 'Course, my daddy didn't get along with much of anybody in the county. But, anyway, Augustus and I...we fell in love. And then he got this job offer from a newspaper up north. That was his dream, you know. To work for some big, Pulitzer Prize-winnin' publication. So, when the offer came, he asked me to marry him and leave Deacon's Crossin'."

"Oh, Aunt Henny," Callie murmured, temporarily forgetting her own heartache in the face of her aunt's obvious pain.

Henny sniffed, tears welling up in her eyes. "I refused him, Callie. I told him it was because of my daddy. He'd never approve of my marryin' the son of a man he swore had tried to make a monkey out of him on more than one occasion. But the truth is, I was scared. Not of bein' disowned, although I would have been if I'd gone off up north. But scared of leavin' my home, my family and friends. Deacon's Crossin' was everythin' to me. I mean, I'd never even traveled out of state! So, I said no to Augustus and he left without me. But he wrote me almost every week for six months, tellin' me how excitin' everythin' was and askin' me to join him. I thought about it, but I never had the gumption to act. I didn't even have the gumption to write him back."

Callie swallowed hard, knowing her own eyes were moist.

"I still love him," Henny continued, tears starting to trickle down her cheeks. "I know that's hard to believe, considerin' how hateful I've been since he came back. But bein' hateful was the only way I could think of to keep him from guessin' how strong my feelin's have been all these years. Because if he guessed that, he'd be bound to ferret out my cowardice. Augustus has a knack for that sort of thing. That's why he's such a fine newspaperman. And I couldn't bear him knowin' I was such a frightened fool, Callie. I couldn't bear him realizin' how unworthy I was of his regard. I just couldn't bear it."

The older woman came very close to breaking down then. Callie gathered her into a hug, stroking her back and making soothing sounds. I should have guessed, she chastised herself. I should have guessed.

Eventually Henny recovered enough to disengage herself from Callie's embrace. She sat up, patting at her hair and fussing with her robe. Although she was still sniffling and snuffling, she was infinitely more composed than she'd been just a few minutes before.

"That's enough about me," she said with a little nod. Her tone was tremulous but determined. "I didn't come in here to talk about me and my mistakes, Callie. I came in here to talk about you and yours. There's two things I've got to know. First of all, do you love Jacob Turner?"

Callie stared at her aunt. There was only one answer she could give. Taking a deep breath, she gave it.

"Yes," she whispered. "With all my heart."

"And second, do you want to be with him?"

Again, there was only one answer. But this time Callie hesitated, thinking about roots and responsibilities.

"No!" her aunt said, apparently divining the direction of her thoughts. "I don't want you considerin' me or P.D. in this. You've put yourself last for six years, Callie. It's time to stop. *Do you want to be with him?*"

Callie nodded. "Yes, Aunt Henny. Oh, yes. I want it more than anything."

"Then you've got to tell him," the older woman stated. She raised one hand like a traffic cop as Callie opened her mouth to protest. "I know. I know. You're scared of what'll happen once you do. Well, there are no guarantees. But I believe Jacob loves you, Callie. Truly, I do. The problem is, I don't think he realizes it. Now, I don't know how much he told you about himself. He certainly didn't tell me much, and I tried pryin' more than once. Still, I got the feelin' he was hidin' some deep hurts. I also got the feelin' he's never had much experience with things like havin' a home, bein' part of a family or fallin' in love. And a man can only act in accordance with his experience until somebody shows him somethin' different."

A sense of hope—something she hadn't felt in many days—suffused Callie. Was it possible? she asked herself, her heart beating much more quickly than normal. Was it possible?

If there was even the tiniest sliver of a chance...

"I've got Jake's address," she said suddenly, finding herself reevaluating the implications of his decision to leave it for her. "It's only a P.O. box—"

"But it's a start."

Callie nodded, her mind now racing as fast as her pulse. "I've got to find him, Aunt Henny," she declared. "I've got to find him and tell him how I feel. And if I have to chase him all over creation to do it, I will!"

"Dammit," Jake muttered, clenching and unclenching his hands. "Dammit."

He'd arrived in Vermont roughly three hours before, after a journey that had started in London and included a protracted stopover in New York. He was now sprawled on the couch in the modest two-room apartment he'd occupied at irregular intervals for the past fifteen years.

He looked like hell and he knew it. He also knew there was very little he could do about it. Sure, a shower and a shave might mean a marginal improvement, but they'd do nothing to alter the bleak look in his eyes or the black circles beneath them. And yes, a good night's sleep would probably work wonders, but how was he supposed to get it? To sleep was to dream and to dream was to see the creamy-skinned face of the brown-haired, hazel-eyed woman who'd haunted him for every minute of every hour of every one of the twelve days since he'd said goodbye to her.

"Callie," Jake said aloud. "Oh, God...Callie."

Memory after memory sliced through him. Each one cut deeper than the one before. They scored his heart and soul like razors.

Jake had honestly believed that he'd built up enough emotional scar tissue over the years to be immune to hurt. He'd learned in the past twelve days that he'd believed wrong. Experience hadn't numbed him. Time hadn't atrophied his ability to feel emotional pain.

His anguish wasn't simply a matter of feeling empty. No, it was more a matter of feeling incomplete at the most basic level. He'd been whole with Callie. For one glorious month, he'd been whole. But now...now he was in pieces. And even if he could put those pieces back together, he'd never be the man he'd been in Deacon's Crossing. Something vital would always be missing. And that something was—

The sound of knuckles rapping against his door yanked Jake back to the present. The distinctive rhythm of the knocking made the identity of his caller very clear.

"Come in, Sam," he called.

The door to his apartment swung open.

"How'd you know it was me?" asked the man who was Jake Turner's landlord, business partner and best friend. Sixty-eight-year-old Sam Swayze stepped into the apartment and elbowed the door shut behind him.

Jake sat up, running a hand through his shaggy hair. "Because nobody else ever comes up here."

"Don't be so sure about that," Sam responded, moving over to the beat-up leather lounge chair next to the couch.

Jake frowned. Cryptic remarks were not Sam Swayze's style. He preferred bulldozer directness. "What's that supposed to mean?" he questioned warily.

Sam shrugged. He sat down, his back ramrod straight. While the passage of time had turned his hair white and put a paunch where there'd once been a washboard-flat belly, it had not yet managed to slump his shoulders or unstiffen his spine. He eyed Jake for a moment, then offered a critique of his appearance that combined language from the barnyard and the barracks.

Jake gave a humorless laugh. "Nice to see you, too."

"I mean it, Jake," Sam emphasized. "When you hauled in here a week ago last Tuesday morning, you looked like hell. And damned if you don't look worse now. You want to tell me what's going on?"

Jake's wariness increased. "Nothing's going on. The trip to England was fine. The commission's a real plum."

"I don't give a damn about England. I want to know what happened in Georgia. Are you going to tell me or not?"

"Not."

Sam said nothing. He didn't have to. The look in his steely gray eyes was eloquent in the extreme.

Jake let nearly a minute go by then swore under his breath. Sam knew. He might not know the who or the where or the when, but Sam knew.

"Is it that obvious?" Jake asked bitterly.

The older man's brows scaled his forehead. "What? That you're eating yourself up from the inside out because of a woman? Yeah. It's that obvious."

"I didn't say anything about a woman."

Sam snorted derisively. "You didn't have to."

Jake closed his eyes for a moment. "I had to leave her," he said, falling back on the litany he'd been reciting over and over to himself for the past twelve days. He opened his eyes and repeated, "I *had* to."

"Why?" The question was blunt.

"Because it never would have worked out."

"Why not?" This one was bludgeoning.

"Dammit, Sam!" Jake exploded. He drew a shuddery breath, struggling for control. When he resumed speaking, his voice was taut. "Callie Barnwell and I are two entirely different kinds of people!"

The older man's eyes narrowed slightly. Other than that, there was no visible reaction to Jake's outburst.

"Callie," he repeated slowly. "That's the niece, right?"

Jake went rigid. "How did you know that?" he demanded.

An odd expression flickered across Sam's face. "I talked to her aunt—Jennie, is it? Or Penny?"

"Henny," Jake supplied tersely. "When?"

"When what?"

"When did you talk to Miss Henny?"

"Weeks ago. I'd called looking for you. But, to tell the truth, I didn't really talk to the lady. Our conversation was more a matter of her yakking and me trying to get a word in whenever she stopped to draw breath."

"Have you spoken to Miss Henny since then?"

Sam shook his head. Again, a peculiar look danced its way across his features.

There was a strained silence. Jake averted his eyes, balling his hands into fists.

"Did you tell her?" Sam asked finally.

"Did I tell who what?"

"Did you tell Callie Barnwell you and she are two entirely different kinds of people and it'd never work out between you?"

Jake looked back at the older man. "Yes," he answered baldly, knowing there was no one else in the world he'd permit to trample on his privacy like this.

"Was this before or after you took her to bed?"

The question was like a stiletto blade. It stabbed straight between Jake's ribs and into his heart.

"Before," he replied. "And...after. I also told her I was going to leave Deacon's Crossing at the end of August and never come back."

"Did you mean it?"

Jake rubbed his face with both palms. Several days' worth of stubble rasped his palms. "Yeah," he said, then tacked on wearily, "I think."

"You think?" Sam's voice was incisive.

"I meant it when I said it," Jake returned. "But then— God, what do you want to hear?" He got up from the couch and began pacing. He wanted to kick something. A door maybe. "Do you want to hear that I was hoping Callie would ask me to stay on? Fine. Yes! I hoped for that. Do you want to hear that it got to the point where I was having fantasies about white lace promises and happily-ever-after endings? All right. I'll admit to that, too. But, dammit! It never would've worked!"

"Why not?"

"For God's sake, Sam! My father was a drunk. My mother's a—a—well, you know what my mother is. And Lord knows what I would have turned out to be if you hadn't come along and kicked my butt into some kind of shape. But just because I'm not addicted to booze or bed hopping doesn't mean I'm capable of giving Callie Barnwell what she deserves."

"It doesn't mean you're not, either."

"Sam—"

"Shut up!" the older man ordered sharply. "You know, maybe I shouldn't have spent so many years kicking your butt. Maybe I should've been trying to knock some sense into that thick skull of yours instead. Assuming that's where your brain's located, of course. Answer me something, Jake. In all the time you spent telling Callie Barnwell why things were never going to work out between the two of you, did you ever let her tell you why she thought they would?"

"She never thought—"

"She got involved with you, didn't she? And judging from what you've said—and haven't said—she's not your usual come-and-go type."

"No," Jake agreed after a moment. "She's not my...usual...type."

"Well then?"

Jake moved slowly back to the couch and sat down. His thoughts were arrowing in a dozen different directions, yet they all kept ending up in the same place.

Was what Sam was suggesting possible? he asked himself.

He'd never questioned why Callie had been willing to give herself to him with such unstinting generosity. Out of ignorance or arrogance, he'd simply accepted what she'd offered.

She'd wanted him. He believed that to the very marrow of his bones. Callie Barnwell had wanted *him*. She'd told him he wasn't her type almost as often as he'd told her she wasn't his, and yet...

Jake sucked in his breath, suddenly seeing how twisted his attitude had been. He couldn't have it both ways. Either Callie was a woman capable of coming through a brief, no-strings affair intact—in which case she *was* his type or, at least, what had been his type—or she wasn't. And if she wasn't capable of it—if she truly *wasn't* his type—then why had she become involved with him? Why had she knowingly opened herself to hurt?

Could it have been for the same reason he dreamed about her by night and fantasized about her by day? Could it have been for the same reason he still tasted her on his lips, still felt her on his skin? Could it have been—

Dear God, he thought, his heart lurching. I love her. All this time I've loved Callie! But after what I've done...

Jake blinked several times, then focused on his longtime mentor. "I've got to go back to Deacon's Crossing," he declared flatly.

"I kind of thought you might," Sam answered. He smiled a little. "It's better this way, you know."

"Better?"

"Better than her coming to you."

It took Jake a few seconds to absorb the implications of this statement. When he combined those implications with his recollection of one cryptic comment and two odd expressions, he came to a stunning conclusion.

"You've talked to Callie," he accused, staring at the older man. "Dammit, Sam, you've talked to her, haven't you?"

Sam nodded, apparently unruffled. "She called yesterday. Funny, I hardly noticed her having an accent at the beginning. But it got stronger and stronger as the conversation went along. By the time she gave me a message, she sounded a whole lot like her aunt."

Jake's breath had wedged at the top of his throat. "What was the message?" He had to fight to get the question out.

"It was real simple," Sam replied. "She has something important to say to you and she intends to say it face-to-face as soon as possible."

The wedge dissolved. Jake's breath came out in a rush. Two phrases from Callie's message reverberated inside his skull.

Something important to say.

Say it face-to-face.

Exactly, love, he thought with tender ferocity.

Then, to Sam, "Why didn't you tell me before?"

The older man shrugged. "Probably for the same reason I made you repair that door you kicked the hole in."

Sam didn't linger more than a couple of minutes after that. While Jake's recollection of most of what was said during those couple of minutes was always pretty hazy, there was a fragment of the conversation that never faded from his memory. It was the question Sam asked as he got up out of the leather lounge chair.

"Just one more thing, Jake."

"Yeah, Sam?" Jake was busy devising scenarios for what he realized was going to be the most important face-to-face encounter of his life. He knew what he wanted—needed— to say to Callie, but he wasn't certain how to say it. The circumstances had to be...well, he had this inexplicable conviction that the circumstances of his return to Caroline Anne Barnwell's life should be as dramatic as his entrance into it.

"What the hell are those white lace promises you said you'd been fantasizing about?"

Twelve

———

Chaos—genteel but genuine—reigned supreme inside the Caroline Anne Barnwell Memorial Library in Deacon's Crossing, Georgia. This was because Petal Conroy had decreed that the facility would be the gathering point for all those participating in that year's Founders' Day Festival historic presentation.

In the midst of the chaos there was one corner of comparative serenity. It was occupied by Callie Barnwell and her aunt.

"You look beautiful, Callie," Henny said fondly, fluffing one of her niece's puffed sleeves. "Just beautiful."

"Thank you, Aunt Henny."

"Now, you're not nervous, are you?"

"About my reading?" Callie laughed a little, plucking at the skirt of her satin-and-lace gown. She wondered if the light-headedness she was experiencing was due to anxiety or oxygen deprivation caused by the tightness of her bodice. "No. I'm not nervous about that."

"Good. Good. And I don't want you to go worryin' about anythin' else, either. There's goin' to be a taxicab waitin' outside your shop to take you to the airport just as soon as you change. You've got your plane ticket to Vermont?"

"Yes." The word caught briefly in Callie's throat. Jake, she thought longingly. *Jake.*

"And your suitcase?"

"Yes."

"I hope you don't mind, but I reopened it after you finished packin' and put in a few extra things. I wanted to make sure you were properly prepared."

Callie flushed from breast to brow at the last word. No, she told herself firmly. There's no way Aunt Henny can know about that. Everything else, yes. But not that!

"Thank you," she managed to say.

Her aunt smiled. "And you've got Jake's address? Not the mailin' one. The livin' one."

Callie nodded, the pearl drop earrings she was wearing dancing against her cheeks. "Yes. Sam Swayze gave it to me when I called. You will thank Mr. Bates again for helping me get his telephone number, won't you?"

Now it was the older woman's turn to color. "I think I could arrange to do that," she said with a coy laugh and fluttery hand movement. "I . . . well, it just so happens that I've invited Augustus to join me and P.D. for Sunday dinner tomorrow." She suddenly looked anxious. "You don't think I was too bold, Callie, do you?"

"What did Mr. Bates say?"

Another fluttery gesture. "To my invitation, you mean?"

"Yes."

Another coy laugh. "Oh, he said he'd be deeply honored to partake of any meal I cooked."

Callie leaned forward and kissed her aunt on the cheek. "Well, then, I don't think you were too bold at all. I think you showed—" she smiled "—gumption."

"I'm just so out of practice at this sort of thing. And after I invited him, I kept rememberin' what Petal Conroy always quotes her late husband as sayin' about forward women. Not that I think Horace really said it. The only opinions he ever had were the ones Petal gave him. But still—''

''Speaking of Petal Conroy,'' Callie interrupted, pressing a gloved hand over her heart. She was desperately trying to keep her mind off what might lie ahead of her. She could only pray that she would demonstrate as much gumption in dealing with Jake Turner as her aunt had shown in dealing with Augustus Bates during the past three days. If the two old lovers weren't completely reconciled yet, they soon would be. ''Is she all right?''

''You mean after that conniption fit she threw when she discovered somebody'd broken in here and made off with one of the costumes for today's historical tableaux? That certainly was a sight to behold, wasn't it?''

''I thought she was having a heart attack.''

''No. No. She was screamin' too much for it to be a heart attack.''

''Who do you think did it?''

Henny sighed. ''I have absolutely no idea. But I heard that whoever he was, he left an exceptionally polite note sayin' the garment was bein' taken for a vital purpose and that it'd be given back in the end.''

''A thief with manners?''

''Well, I don't know if it's really thievin' if there's a written promise that what's been taken is goin' to be brought back,'' the older woman demurred.

''Mmm.'' Callie gave her hair a pat. It had been styled into an elegant upsweep by none other than Janie Mae Winslow. The coiffure was quite lovely. Callie just wished the veteran beauty queen hadn't insisted on coating it with something she'd blithely referred to as ''hair cement.''

''Have you seen P.D.?'' Henny asked abruptly.

''P.D.?'' Callie blinked. ''Why no. Not for hours.''

''Did you think he was actin' kind of peculiar at breakfast?''

Callie frowned, trying to remember. In all honesty she hadn't paid much attention to her half brother's behavior that morning. In point of fact she hadn't paid much attention to anything beyond the mixture of anticipation and apprehension roiling within her.

"No more peculiarly than usual, Aunt Henny," she said finally.

The older woman clucked her tongue. "He got a telephone call yesterday—did I tell you? It was after you'd left for your shop. I don't know who it was or what was said. The conversation lasted about ten minutes. I asked him about it afterward. Curiosity, you know. And he looked me straight in the eye and swore it'd been a wrong number. Then he went tearin' off sayin' he had to see Seth Avery." She raised her brows. "You don't think he could be up to somethin', do you?"

"You nervous, Jake?"

Jake forked his fingers through his hair and gave P.D. Barnwell a wry look. He and the teenager were standing around the corner from the outdoor stage that had been put up in the park across from the Caroline Anne Barnwell Memorial Library. He couldn't see what was going on, but he could hear Augustus Bates's amplified voice and the applause of the gathered crowd.

"Nervous doesn't begin to describe how I feel right now, kid," he answered frankly.

"Scared spitless, huh?"

"Worse."

"It's goin' to work, Jake. I just know it's goin' to."

"God, I hope so," Jake returned fervently. The idea that had come to him less than forty-eight hours before was beginning to seem less and less inspired and more and more idiotic. He'd wanted to do something dramatic to demonstrate his feelings for Caroline Anne Barnwell. Something romantic. Unfortunately he was becoming increasingly convinced that there was a very fine line between dramatically romantic and downright ridiculous. He was also well on his way to believing that he was on the verge of stumbling over that line.

"Jake?"

"Yeah, P.D.?" He scratched under his left arm.

"I'm awful sorry about the smell. Me and Seth tried to find somethin' in your size that didn't stink of mothballs but we couldn't."

"That's okay, kid," Jake assured the teenager, scratching his right thigh. He'd become more or less inured to the peculiar odor emanating from the old-fashioned garments he had on. He just wished he could figure out how to ignore the itchiness of the fabric from which they'd been made!

"It was Seth's idea to spray on the air freshener. He thought it might help," P.D. went on. "Some dumb notion that was. It's almost as dumb as Janie Mae Winslow tellin' Stella to rub baby oil on her turkey so it'd shine on stage while she was stuffin' it. I swear, that bird flew right out of Stella's hands durin' the preliminary talent competition and landed smack dab in one of the judge's laps. She still made finalist, though. I figure she probably got points for stayin' poised instead of fallin' to pieces. But, anyway. I apologize for the air freshener. I think it made the smell of that old suit even worse than it was to start with."

"Well, you deserve points for getting me these clothes. I don't know how you managed it."

"Oh, me and Seth kind of temporarily borrowed them."

"Well, I owe you, P.D.," Jake said sincerely, clapping the teenager on the shoulder. "I owe you big."

P.D. suddenly flushed. He dropped his eyes and scuffed his foot against the ground. "I was mighty glad when you called yesterday, you know," he muttered gruffly.

The crowd in the park was cheering. But Jake ignored the noise, focusing on Callie's half brother. His instincts told him that P.D. was preparing himself to say something very important.

"You were?" he asked, watching P.D. closely.

The teenager looked up, his jaw jutting, his eyes chal-
enging. "Yeah, I was," he declared. "'Cuz if you hadn't
alled...or come back...I was fixin' to come after you with
shotgun."

Jake sustained P.D.'s gaze steadily for several seconds,
etting the teenager see he understood the emotions behind
hese harsh words and accepted them.

"You wouldn't've blown a hole in the ceiling this time,
ould you?" he said finally.

P.D. shook his head decisively. "No, sir. I wouldn't've."

Jake smiled crookedly. "A man's got to do what a man's
ot to do, huh, Palmer Dean?"

The teenager's expression eased. "Yeah," he affirmed.

"Well, sometimes figuring out what's got to be done takes
lot longer than it should, kid," Jake confessed. "Say, for
astance, that the man who ought to be doing the doing is
—a—"

The teenager supplied a noun modified by several color-
ul adjectives.

Jake gave a wry chuckle. "Right. Well, that kind of man
eems to need a few swift kicks in the butt—or whacks to the
ead—to help him understand what's right."

"You get kicked?"

"And whacked."

"By that Mr. Swayze?"

"Yeah."

P.D. frowned. "He's not your kin, is he?"

"No. Not really," Jake answered. "But he's the closest
hing to family I've ever had."

Callie's half brother grinned suddenly. "You know, I just
et that'll change after you get done playin' Harriman Gage
ack from the grave. Which reminds me of somethin'. I
on't think you can go takin' the part of a man who's been
rowned to death without bein' just a little bit wet...do
ou?"

Callie took a deep breath, preparing to launch into the
inal sentences of her recitation.

Everything had gone flawlessly so far, despite the fact tha[t] she'd been having a great deal of trouble keeping track [of] her text. She didn't want to think about the happily ever a[f]ter her long-dead ancestress had never had. All she wante[d] to do was to think about the enduring love that might [be] hers if she had the courage to reach out and claim it.

Still, she'd persevered.

Augustus Bates had helped by giving her an absolute[ly] charming introduction—an introduction which had i[n]cluded a few graceful allusions to her aunt. The fact that th[e] gathered throng had responded to the sight of her gown wit[h] delighted ooohs and aaahs had bolstered her nerves, too.

As she'd approached the climax of her presentation, Ca[l]lie had started hearing sighs and sobs from the audienc[e.] Looking out at the crowd now, she saw that more than a fe[w] women were dabbing at their cheeks with handkerchief[s.] She spotted Bernice, the waitress from Earle's All You Ca[n] Eat, openly crying on her employer's shoulder.

"Oh, boo-hoo-hooooo," Bernice blubbered. "This is s[o] sa-a-a-a-d."

Callie wrenched her attention away from the weepin[g] waitress, dimly registering that there seemed to be some kin[d] of disturbance in the back of the crowd. She straightene[d] her shoulders and stiffened her spine.

"And so, I will put away my dreams of white lace prom[i]ises and devote myself to doin' good," she quoted, co[n]sciously exaggerating her drawl. "Although my heart an[d] arms may be empty, my life will be—"

"Caroline Anne!" a resonant male voice suddenly calle[d] out.

Callie froze. She knew that voice. She knew it with ever[y] fiber of her being.

"Jake?" she whispered, staring out at the rapidly par[t]ing crowd. Although a sudden rush of tears threatened t[o] blur her vision, she could see that people were clearing [a] path for a tall, tawny-haired man clad in an old-fashione[d] suit of clothes.

The man came to a halt directly in front of the stage, gazing up at her with the most vivid pair of blue-green eyes he'd ever seen. And the look in those vivid eyes was so full of love it made her heart stand still for just a moment.

"Jake?" she repeated. What was he doing here? she wondered dizzily. How had he come to be dressed like a man from the 1870s? And why in the name of heaven did it look as though someone had dumped a bucket of water over him?

"It's me, Caroline Anne!" Jake boomed, spreading his arms. Two of the buttons on his shirt popped off. He didn't care about that any more than the fact that he was soaking wet thanks to a surprise dousing from P.D. All he cared about was the slender brown-haired woman who was standing above him looking like a stunned angel in lace. "Harriman Gage!"

"H-Harriman G-Gage?" Callie felt faint. Her brain was in a whirl. She said the first thing that occurred to her. "But, you're drowned!"

"That's the old version. In this version, I survived because I know how to swim. In this version, the low-down Yankee bastard and his beautiful Southern belle live happily ever after."

Jake mounted the stage in an athletic leap. Three strides brought him to where Callie was standing. He took her in his arms, gazing down into her eyes for one sweetly searing moment.

And then . . . he kissed her.

Compared with many of the other kisses they'd shared, it was very chaste. Yet it contained such a quality of cherishing that it made Callie quiver to the core of her soul.

"Jake," she sighed blissfully when he finally lifted his mouth from hers. It seemed to her that the single syllable of his name defined all she understood of hope and happiness.

Jake cupped her face. "I came back to Deacon's Crossing because nothing—not even my own blind stupidity—could keep me away from you, sweetheart," he told her,

then paused. When he resumed speaking, the intensity of h
emotions frayed the edges of his words. "I love you, Call
Barnwell. I love you in every way a man can love a woman.

"And I love you, Jake Turner," Callie responded, liftir
one hand and stroking his cheek. She felt him tremble at h
touch. A sense of triumphant tenderness filled her. "I lo
you so much it'd take a lifetime to tell you."

"Forgive me?"

"If there's anything to forgive, I've forgotten it."

There was a breathless pause.

"Will you marry me?" Jake asked solemnly.

"Oh, yes," Callie answered simply.

And then . . . *she* kissed *him*.

The crowd erupted into cheers. It was, after all, an hi
toric occasion.

Callie was still kissing Jake when he swept her up ar
carried her off the stage and into their future.

After more than a century of setbacks and spinelessnes
at least one female member of the Barnwell family turne
out to be very, very lucky in love—and she knew it.

Caroline Anne Barnwell married Jacob MacNeil Turne
one month later.

Palmer Dean Barnwell the Third gave the bride away. Th
recently engaged Miss Henrietta Penelope Barnwell a
tended as her maid of honor.

Sam Swayze served as best man.

Among those present at the wedding were the maid o
honor's fiancé, Mr. Augustus Bates, the winner of th
year's Founders' Day Festival pageant, Miss Stella Aver
and a flower-festooned dog of indeterminate breedir
named Buttercup.

While the ceremony was small, the reception that fo
lowed filled the Barnwell house to overflowing. Yet, d
spite the demands for their time and attention, th
newlyweds managed to steal a few moments for then
selves.

A brief, brushing kiss.

"I love you, wife."

A soft, sensuous caress.

"I love you, husband."

An exchange of intimate smiles followed by husky whispers.

"You're still not my type, sweetheart."

"No?"

"No. You're my heart and soul. You're my home and my family."

"You're everything I ever wanted."

Another kiss, longer and more lingering than the first. Another caress, possessive as well as passionate.

"We're going to make a wonderful life together here in Deacon's Crossing."

"Is that a promise?"

Jake took Callie into his arms and held her tight against him. "It's a white lace promise," he assured her. "And it's guaranteed to last forever."

* * * * *

You'll flip . . . your pages won't!
Read paperbacks *hands-free* with

Book Mate · I

The perfect "mate" for all your romance paperbacks
Traveling • Vacationing • At Work • In Bed • Studying
• Cooking • Eating

Perfect size for all standard paperbacks, this wonderful invention makes reading a pure pleasure! Ingenious design holds paperback books OPEN and FLAT so even wind can't ruffle pages — leaves your hands free to do other things. Reinforced, wipe-clean vinyl-covered holder flexes to let you turn pages without undoing the strap . . . supports paperbacks so well, they have the strength of hardcovers!

Pages turn WITHOUT opening the strap.

SEE-THROUGH STRAP

Reinforced back stays flat.

Built in bookmark

BOOK MARK

BACK COVER HOLDING STRIP

10" x 7¼", opened.
Snaps closed for easy carrying, too